Notes For Elijah

R.R. LaPerle

iUniverse, Inc.
New York   Bloomington

Notes For Elijah

iUniverse books may be ordered through booksellers or by contacting:

iUniverse
1663 Liberty Drive
Bloomington, IN 47403
www.iuniverse.com
1-800-Authors (1-800-288-4677)

ISBN: 978-1-4401-0348-3 (pbk)

ISBN: 978-1-4401-0349-0 (ebk)

Printed in the United States of America

iuniverse rev. date: 6/24/2009

Notes For Elijah

Angles of light, curve of the planet and composition of the atmosphere.

This is science, in every dawn and dusk.

Chapter One

Science

Kate smiled as she returned the pen to paper; "You, my mysterious friend," she wrote, "are like the color in the view before me, challenging description while defying explanation."

Stopping again to gaze at the horizon and gather her thoughts, a smile slowly developed as she recalled part of a conversation from years before. "Such are those things," she ended, "that I know I do not know."

Signing the note and sealing it in the usual manner, inside a plastic sandwich bag, Kate would leave it tacked in the same place as the other notes she had left over the years, just in case the intended recipient should ever return to this place.

The view Kate looked out upon as she finished her writing was to her without compare. The seasonal result of the sun's low angle on the western facing slopes of the Sangre De Cristo was truly breathtaking this time of year. On this particular day, it even made the two-hour drive and the thirty minute ride on horseback seem a trivial effort. Two years had passed since she had come to this place and, at least for the moment, being back seemed perfectly timed.

The inspiration to make this particular trip from Albuquerque stemmed from an article that she had read in the morning paper. Kate found herself smiling earlier that morning while reading the somewhat obscure announcement, and in an uncharacteristic, spur of the moment sort of decision she phoned her office and told her boss that she had decided to use a vacation day, which she did actually need to get about using since she still had more time coming to her than she knew she could use in the remaining months of the calendar year.

Feeling good about her decision, she phoned her father to tell him she was going to take a drive up to visit him. This would be a perfect day to reflect she thought, while sipping her coffee at the kitchen table.

That such printings of news can tend to radically change the course of one's day should not be considered surprising. The first discovery about a drastic decline in a stock price, a familiar photo appearing in the obituary section, or even an ominous weather forecast is sometimes enough to tip the scales on an otherwise evenly balanced attitude.

There are those that prefer to postpone listening to any news broadcasts or reading newspapers until *after* the workday. This way, the potential for any kind of disturbing information actually interfering with the necessary focus of the day is, at least, minimized. Others, though, absolutely must know what's going on, locally and nationally, as a first order of business upon waking. Hence, the early news, the pre-dawn newspaper delivery, and, the clock radio set to a 24 hour news station. Kate was clearly among the latter. Being a journalist, after all, news was her life, and no day could properly begin without the ingestion of every worthy word, and not only in the "Albuquerque Star", her employer, but quite often the New York Times and Washington Post as well.

Much of what she read each morning was already somewhat familiar to her since she rarely failed to give a quick scan of the rough layout of the morning edition before she left work each evening. The particular article that caught her attention on this morning, however, hadn't been noticed the evening before. It was a simple announcement about a new museum dedication in the nation's capitol, but, as the written word can often do, it spawned a floodgate of memories, and it would definitely serve as the track changing intersection on this day.

This would be a perfect time, she thought, as she enjoyed the beauty of the natural vista she had discovered so many years ago, to remember and appreciate her own experience with how life could change so dramatically without warning, and there was no more appropriate place, she was sure, for such reflection than 'her' place.

Kate was thinking back to when she first discovered this high grassy clearing. It was on one of her pioneering rides just before her fourteenth birthday. It was a clear autumn day, she reminisced, and as she approached the edge of the clearing that first time, she observed the "Blood Of Christ" mountains reflecting *so* crimson in the late day, post equinox, sunlight. It was a spectacle she would never forget, and easy to understand how it was that the Spanish settlers came to name these mountains that she had taken, prior to that moment, for granted for as long as she could remember.

For the next few years, she would come to this place as though it was her own, often trying to duplicate what she considered the perfect meeting of landscape and light with paints or, occasionally, just attempting to put the right words in verse in the hope of visually, or verbally, capturing the simple essence of the slogan which so appropriately adorned each license plate in the state; "New Mexico - Land Of Enchantment".

On a warm day in August, just prior to the start of her senior year of high school, Kate was lying in the cool shade of the Aspen near the edge of that meadow, brooding about having to give up a precious portion of the remaining vacation days to attend summer school. It was another in an endless chain of reasons for her to be less than cheerful, not that Kate was ever thought to be an especially sad person. She just seemed to spend more time than most worrying about things that would probably be of little concern to the average teenager. While a very attractive girl by any standard, serious would probably have been a word many of her friends would have chosen first if asked for a condensed description of her. Fun would most likely have been much further down on the list of considerations.

She was all too aware, as she lay there contemplating the premature end of her vacation, that had she put more effort into science class during the second half of the year, she wouldn't be faced with this problem. But then, had she taken World History instead, as she originally intended, she might not be in this predicament either.

Actually, Kate didn't think that Physical Science itself was that bad. The fact that she drew Mr. Talbot for a teacher, the man known throughout the school for his ability to speak, non-stop, for an entire class without the slightest fluctuation in volume or pitch, was the proverbial short straw. The unfortunate coincidence that science class came at the end of the day was, in no small way, also a contributing factor. Of course, Kate's day started earlier than that of most other kids anyway. She had the responsibility of caring for two horses which she talked her father into boarding, plus Sanchez. It was the boarding, though, which accounted for her only source of income, most of which was going into her savings account.

Well, for whatever the reason, the fact that she got a 'D' for a final grade in Physical Science was true, and the principal, Mr. Breen, convinced her father that it would be a good idea to take the class over in order to make up the grade since only the higher of the two would be counted in the overall cumulative average. It would, assuming she could do better the second time, eliminate the 'D' from her record, which, according to Mr. Breen, could be a definite plus in the college applications. Since

Mr. Talbot was away on vacation for the whole month of July, it was arranged that the make up class would be offered in the middle two weeks of August, for four hours each day.

With the eve of day one at hand, even the meadow escape offered little comfort. Thinking about how Mr. Talbot could possibly make Physical Science more interesting than he had during the school year, and how he could possibly help her to concentrate on the subject matter any better than he did the first time dominated her attention, even though she went there seeking some last minute peace of mind. In typical form for Kate, her last free day was, indeed, half gone rather than half remaining. After all, she kept coming back to the uncontestable fact that there were so many other things she could be doing with her time, things that everyone else her age might be doing, if she wasn't going to be stuck in school for the next couple of weeks.

The only positive that Kate could come up with, and it was a stretch, was that the class was scheduled to be in the morning, from 8:30 to 12:30, so her chances of staying awake at that time the day were quite improved. Now, if by some chance her teacher learned to speak in more than one tone over the summer, well, there was a remote possibility that she makes it through and actually gets a better grade.

Sanchez was aware that this was not a good day for his master. He was good about knowing things like that, so he seemed to purposefully stay away from her while she was lying there. Even though he had the cuffs on, which Kate always felt a bit guilty about using, he managed to kind of hop over to the tall grass at the edge of the field and was busy munching while she contemplated her fate. The cuffs, which Sanchez was forced to wear when he wasn't tied up, kept him from wandering off when no one was watching him. Kate learned the importance of this apparatus the hard way when she ended up walking the long downhill trek home after Sanchez wandered all the way back to his barn from this place while she napped one afternoon.

July, she thought, just flew by, and August was mostly gone. "What happened to the vacation so looked forward to all those months?" she wondered. The day to go to the school and pick up a text and confirm her registration had arrived, and summer, for all practical purposes, was ending. Immediately following the two weeks of summer school, of course, would be the new school year, and even though Kate looked forward to finally being a senior, to finally enjoy the anticipated benefits that went along with that status, she still wasn't ready to go back to the routine of six hours of class five days every week, plus homework.

Every high school year, she would admit if pressed, turned out to be better than expected. But, her bleak outlook tended to keep expectations low. As much as Kate disliked leaving the 'oldest' status of Houghton Elementary School for the freshman rank at Theodore Roosevelt High, she did actually enjoy the change. That first year passed rather quickly because everything was new and she was so busy finding her way around, getting used to the new teachers, and meeting a lot of kids from the surrounding towns. It was something of an adventure.

Sophomore year seemed much longer somehow. The work was harder, and most of the friends she had made the first year were not in her classes. But, strictly from the social perspective, it was still superior to the first.

Junior year, while it definitely seemed the longest, still was not quite as bad as she thought it would be. She had very few of her friends in her classes. Her teachers, except for Ms. Turner (French), were all pretty bad, and of course there was the constant struggle in Science.

It was such a relief to finally get to summer vacation. It just couldn't be possible, she thought, that it was time to go back. With that thought, Kate looked at her watch and realized she would have to hurry to get back at the time she told her dad she would meet him for the ride to school.

By the time Kate got Sanchez unsaddled and was just ready to put him back in the corral, her father came walking out from the house toward the barn.

"I'm all set to go, Dad!" she called out, figuring he was about to tell her that they had to be on their way.

"Well," her father began, "there really isn't anywhere to go. At least, not for today".

"I don't have to register, or pick up the book for class tomorrow?"

"As a matter of fact, it doesn't appear you *have* any class tomorrow. I guess they are having a bit of trouble getting someone to take you on, Katelynn," her father answered with a smile. He usually reserved the pleasure of using her whole first name strictly for philosophical or sarcastic moments. She wasn't yet sure exactly which this was.

"Are you saying there won't *be* any make up class?" she asked, unable to mask her excitement.

"I'm not certain, sweetheart. All I know is Mr. Breen called and said that you are the only one still registered for the make-up class at the moment because several of the other students have already made a change in plans," her father explained. "He apologized for letting us know last minute, but Mr. Talbot canceled the class in order to extend his vacation back east. I guess Mr. Breen thought that he could get Mr. Talbot to tutor you individually sometime after he got back, but before the beginning of school. Unfortunately, he is just now realizing that there won't be enough time for that."

"Well, I sure hate to hear that, Dad," Kate smirked with sarcasm.

The thought of her and Mr. Talbot *alone* in a classroom for any length of time during a summer afternoon had not even occurred to her before this. She had just assumed, of course, that other kids would be taking the class along with her, maybe even some from the next school district since her high school was a regional school, and the biggest in the county. It now struck her that if she had known it was even possible to be taking the eight week class alone with Mr. Talbot, well, that would surely have made a much bigger challenge for her father and Mr. Breen to talk her into taking this course just to improve her chances of getting into a better college.

Kate wasn't totally convinced that college was in her future anyway, although she feared discussing that possibility with anyone. She knew that anything short of finishing college would be considered very disappointing to her dad. He had some ideas about her being a veterinarian, because she liked animals so much. But, at times, when she thought about how long people have go to school for a career like that, well, fortunately it was a decision that didn't have to be made for awhile. She had often wished, though, that she could somehow make a career out of her love for drawing or writing, but kept this to herself for fear of being ridiculed about such foolish aspirations.

Kate's dad told her that there would be a meeting with Mr. Breen the next day to discuss what options might still be available to take the make-up class, but she barely heard any of that as she was running back toward the house to call Mallory. She couldn't wait to tell her the good news, after all, Mallory was the one she had complained to about this whole summer school situation for the past six weeks.

Mallory lived in town, in a sprawling, modern house. Her father was the minister of the First Congregational Church that Kate and her dad attended. It was in this church that Kate and Mallory first sang together in the choir, and here that Kate first understood the difference in the range and richness of Mallory's voice as compared to her own. Within the cloak of 15 various choir voices, even at the age of nine, Mallory was this constant right that the other voices would rise to and fall off of. Not standing out by volume, but recognizable as the right pitch within the clamor.

Mallory was Kate's best friend. They had known each other since Kindergarten and became best friends during fifth grade. It was a friendship, some would say, which thrived on their differences rather than what they had in common. For a minister's daughter, Mallory was known to be a bit on the wild side. While she was rather slight in stature, she was perfectly proportioned, and *always* stylish. Kate often joked that even Mal's pajamas had designer labels.

Kate, on the other hand, was more the flannel shirt and jeans type, athletically built, and considered by most to be something of an introvert.

"As with any relationship," Kate's dad once said, "some strength comes from the mix, and not the duplication." Although she didn't quite grasp this when she first heard it, Kate came to embrace the simple logic of how true this was, particularly as it applied to her and Mallory. She knew, though, that when her father had said it he was speaking about he and her mother of course.

Except for the photographs around the house, and the stories her father would tell now and then, Kate could never feel any real connection to her mother. She had died before any lasting memories had a chance to be born. For her, it was as though she never existed, and for her dad, who would still speak to her on occasion as though she were actually listening, it was like she was only away temporarily. Not that he walked around talking to her ghost, or pretended that she was still in the house. It was only when he was really flustered, especially when he was nearing the end of his rope with one or another of Kate's antics, that he would turn to either accuse "Mary

Jane" (more often using "M.J.") of having "left before
the thrill of child rearing," or to seek her guidance with
questions which he had trouble answering himself.

In the twelve years of single parenting, her dad never
dated. He never even spoke of the idea, and although this
seemed normal when she was younger, it was something
that Kate now believed to be partly her fault. Maybe
bringing her up was too demanding for him to think of
himself at all, or perhaps he thought that someone else
might have threatened her relationship with him. It was
something she hoped to discuss with him one day when
the time was right, but whenever the thought occurred to
her, it seemed like something that was just too awkward
to angle into the conversation.

Dad had immersed himself in his work during the
years following Mom's death, and although Kate didn't
fully understand what exactly he did for work, she knew
that he was an engineer, and that clients would hire him
to review or create blueprints, or to look at parcels of
land to determine how to locate roads and larger building
developments.

She had long understood that, as much as he always
seemed so busy, he had control of his own schedule,
and this provided the luxury of having him present at
virtually every recital, softball game or horse competition
for as long as she could remember.

Kate managed to coax her dad into a quick ride over
to Mallory's, and the discussion on the way over mostly
oriented around the possible options that the principal,
Mr. Breen, would come up with for making up this class.
Kate was dying to tell her father that it was perfectly

fine with her to forget the whole thing. She didn't mind having the 'D' factored into her total grade average, even though her dad convinced her that since it was in science it could be the difference between getting accepted to, or getting turned down by, a good college. It wouldn't seem to be such a tragic waste of time and energy, at least in *her* mind, if she decided to just attend the local community college for a couple of years while she figured out what it was she was meant to do with her life.

Of course, she didn't actually tell her father this. She just nodded at his predictions about what kind of options the principal would probably suggest the next day. But, when she got out of the car at Mallory's, she couldn't even remember one of the possible scenarios her father talked about. This was not a rare occurrence. Kate had the ability to "join a whole 'nother world" her dad would often say. But not having paid attention to this particular conversation proved to be inconvenient when Mallory, upon opening the front door, asked what she thought would happen next. All Kate could say, even after the long pause spent thinking about what her dad had told her in the car was "Well, I have no idea. With any luck at all, the class will be canceled and I'll be told that there won't be any way of taking it before school starts."

"Do you think that's possible?" asked Mallory.

"Well, let me think, Mal. You are as familiar as anyone with my sort of luck. It should be about as possible as Daniel asking me to the Homecoming Dance next month."

"You know as well as anyone, my friend, that the only one Danny Boy notices, that is besides himself of course, is Eden Lyric," Mallory shot back. "But then, that's really what you like about him isn't it?"

"It was sarcasm, Mal, strictly sarcasm; and what do you mean it's what I like about him?"

"I know you, Kate. You always get distant as soon as you know a boy wants to get close to you. It's like you are more comfortable chasing a boy that you know you can't have."

"Wow, Mal, it really is *such* a good thing that you are musically gifted, because your feel for psychology is truly twisted. That is just *so* much bull."

Kate was convinced that life would be considerably improved if the most popular boy in the whole school, and the shoe-in for President of the senior class, Daniel Pratt, suddenly realized his ongoing error in judgment, broke up with Eden, and began to pursue her instead. While this existed as a remote possibility, even if only to Kate, there was little chance of Mallory fixing her up with any of *her* friends.

"Sorry Kate, I don't know where that came from," Mal apologized. "While we're on the subject of boys, though, am I going to have to tell Keith that you won't come to see the band play at "The Rack" next Friday?"

"I don't know Mal. I told you to tell him that I wasn't interested."

"Yes, you told me. But I just don't understand how you can judge him without giving the poor guy a chance. He really seems to have a thing for you, Kate, and he's definitely cute. Besides, we're not talking marriage here."

"I promise I'll go with you to see Randy's band one of these Fridays, Mal. I've just been kind of busy is all."

Randy was the current light of Mallory's life. He played lead guitar in a band that called themselves "The Hombres." They mostly played the '18 and under' circuit one night a week at one or the other of the local hangouts in the next town, "The Rack", or "The Howling Coyote". On the rare occasion, Mallory would take the stage for a song with Randy, and by the enthusiastic response typically rendered by the audience, this would provide one of the musical highlights of their evening. There was an unmistakable chemistry between the two when on stage, and Randy seemed to find his strength playing haunting undertones to Mal's heart piercing ballads, her voice honed and polished over several years of choir participation.

Unfortunately, these duets were pretty rare, and since Randy was responsible for putting the band together, and none of the other members seemed interested in assuming the lead singer role, he had taken up the challenge.

What would probably have been considered by most kids Mal's age to be a pretty decent sounding band for the area was, therefore, severely hampered by the limits of Randy's vocal range. With the exception of Pink Floyd's "The Wall", which would at times consume half of a set on its own and required little more than a speaking voice, the band's repertoire mostly consisted of music loud enough to offset Randy's limitations in both range and pitch.

Mallory was always somewhat reluctant to take the stage on these nights, but ended up doing it either because of the audience prompting, or the simple fact that she loved the back-up that Randy provided, and was convinced it made her sound so much more talented than she felt she was. The fact that she had not succumbed to the pleading for her to join the Hombres as a full time member was, on occasion, still a sticking point with both Randy and Wayne, but she strongly resisted this temptation on the grounds that the dating, plus practicing and playing a few nights a week, had the potential to provide more time together than what might be good for the relationship, so she remained committed to her own band. And while they had not yet had a 'paid' performance, they did play a few back-yard parties and, much to Mal's surprise, received high praise from those in attendance. She was very comfortable singing with the three boys she had known since grade school, and felt that the music they played came across as very "fluid' in her description. At the same time, however, she realized it was never going to be record worthy. This, of course, presented a conflict when thinking about the 'Battle of the Bands' competition, because, while she truly felt that her (yet un-named) band was competitive with those she saw in prior years, it wasn't by any means a sure winner.

Meanwhile, the highlights of each "Hombres" gig, at least on the nights without the Randy / Mallory duets, were typically provided by the keyboard player, who was known to everyone as "Cola". Once each show they would even reach back for a revival of "96 Tears" just to feature him and, fortunately, it was yet another number that required very little in the way of vocals.

Keith was new to "The Hombres." He was the youngest in the band, and the only one still in high school.

Randy and the drummer, Sean, had just graduated, while Cola was in the graduating class ahead of Randy.

Wayne Hayes picked up the nickname Cola in high school after winning a bet by tossing back two quarts of Pepsi in thirteen seconds. He might have done it faster if the stuff came out of the bottles any quicker than that. He had one of those throats that just seemed to open completely when required. Anyway, the nickname stuck because of the spectacle he presented with all that foam gushing out of his nose and mouth for a good minute after the contest was over.

Because of the unintended, Joe Cocker like, contortions Wayne would exhibit during some of the more difficult keyboard solos, the out of the ordinary name definitely seemed more appropriate than the one given him by his parents. 'Wayne' just wouldn't seem to fit him anymore. It was as though someone had advised him early on in his musical schooling that audience appreciation is enhanced by the credible appearance of pain on the part of the artist.

Actually, Keith was the only one still in school at all, since the three older members had convinced themselves that there was more money to be made in playing music than investing in a college degree. Of course, to keep their cars on the road, each needed other part time employment. For each the only serious job, though, was playing in the band. Besides, even if they never got discovered, the once a week gig kept the needle on the fun meter well to the right.

Keith had transferred to Roosevelt at the beginning of the last school year, as a Junior. Kate had noticed him in her Biology class, but didn't really pay much attention to him. After all, this happened to be the one class that she shared with Daniel. Of course Daniel paid even less attention to her than she paid to Keith, so the natural balance of male/female chemistry seemed in order, at least in the microcosm that was known as Biology class.

When Mallory told her that she thought this new kid liked her, toward the end of the last school year, Kate said she thought that he looked a bit like a tough guy, not the imposing, muscle bound, cigarette hanging from the mouth type, but the sort of scruffy hair, collar up look, and the 'don't really *care* how I look' sort of attitude. This, of course, was exactly what Mallory liked about the boy. But, naturally, comparing him to Daniel, as Kate compared all potential dates, he was just too different in her mind.

By the time Kate heard her name echoing up the stairs, and over the music playing on the stereo, it was the third time Mallory's mother had yelled for her. She tumbled off the bed trying to untangle her legs and get up at the same time. By the time she got to the bedroom door Mrs. Chase had already climbed the stairs and was standing on the other side as she opened it.

"Are you kids deaf?" she asked.

"Really sorry Mrs. Chase!" Kate cowered. "We were so deep in conversation I never heard you calling."

"Your dad is outside waiting in the car, dear. Were you supposed to be picked up now?"

"Oh my God Mal!" Kate blurted out as she glanced at her watch. "It's 7:00! I told my dad to pick me up at 6:45 for dinner. How could three hours go by like that?"

she said as she made her way out the door and down the stairs, voice trailing in the descent.

The time had passed in a blur of cassette tapes, nail painting, news about who broke up with who and laughing about what Mr. Talbot's summer class *might* have been like had it not been canceled.

"Well, I'd be willing to bet a good bit of it was spent putting that fancy pearl coat on those nails," Mallory's mother chimed in as she followed Kate down the stairs.

Kate looked at her nails and for just a fleeting moment, while she turned to yell goodbye to Mallory, wondered how Mrs. Chase could possibly notice something like fresh nail polish on her as she was running for the door in a partially lit hallway.

"See Ya, Mal!" she yelled up the stairs.

"You think about next Friday!" was the response coming from the upstairs room as Kate cleared the door in a trot to her father's car.

'It's a hard knock life, *for us*. It's a hard knock life *for us*' was the tune wafting through the door of Kate's bedroom the next morning. There was no doubt in her mind that sleep had come to an unwelcome end once she recognized the all too familiar tune. This was not music which could be ignored for a few extra 'in between sleep and waking' minutes.

Dad loved the show tunes, and he had at least a hundred of them in his collection. But it seemed that the Annie tunes tended to get more of the morning play. She figured he must have found them to be either an invigorating, or a just plain upbeat way to start the day.

Kate, on the other hand, found waking to the "Annie" tunes comparable to what she imagined a Chinese water torture to be. And, as with the water torture, she suspected there was little chance that it would grow on her, as he often suggested. She did, however, share an appreciation for his latest addition to that particular collection. Several of the tunes on his soundtrack of "Les Miserables" had quickly become some of her favorite songs. But, naturally, he didn't seem to give that one as much play.

"Time for breakfast, Kate!" yelled her father from the kitchen.

"Coming." was all she could muster in reply, still buried in her pillow.

"I hope so. I would hate to see this omelet get cold."

It is understandably unlikely that an image of eggs, however prepared, would provide the slightest of incentive for a teenage girl to rush the transition time from deep sleep to a full vertical position, yet it seems a popular ploy among fathers. Kate always imagined that her dad woke up every morning thinking about what to have for breakfast. She did not. The egg and cheese visual during the first waking moments was to her, at best, unappealing.

At 6:15 on a summer morning, there were probably not many people Kate's age on the rise. But, there were horses to walk and feed, and Kate was quite used to the routine. She never did, however, share the same feelings as her father about a complete breakfast being a necessary beginning to a good day. Her appetite generally didn't awaken for an hour or two after her body went into motion, and this created the same dilemma almost every morning. She would either pick at the French toast, or eggs, or oatmeal, forcing it down just to keep from looking ungrateful for the effort, or pretend there was absolutely no time and just swallow some juice while running through the kitchen on her way to the barn. Today she tried the 'no time' maneuver, but was stopped well short of the exit and reminded that there was plenty of time.

"The horses aren't going anywhere, Katelynn, and there's no clock in the barn so they probably won't even realize you're late."

"Well, I wanted to get through early so I can get ready for our meeting at school," Kate cleverly offered.

"That meeting is at 10:30, sweetheart. Do you think you need that much time to get ready?"

He was clearly ahead on all cards after the first round, and although there were one or two excuse strategies left to explore, Kate decided that taking a seat at the table and eating some portion of what was offered seemed the easier option.

The time spent every morning with the horses was often very productive thinking time for Kate. Usually, this was the time of day when important plans were laid out, major decisions made and, sometimes, even potential boyfriends evaluated. This particular morning, however, the time was spent wondering what Mr. Breen was going to suggest, and mapping out the strategies for countering any of the possible alternatives. This was, by all means, a deep thought kind of morning. Even the horses took notice of how aloof Kate seemed to be.

Sanchez was quite accustomed to a lot of attention during this time of day. Most mornings he listened to Kate's problems while she thought out loud. Of course, he seemed to understand that he wasn't expected to offer any help, but he kept his ears high to show he was listening just the same.

Today, except for the trance-like "good morning boy," there was only silence. Sanchez, not at all happy with the lack of enthusiasm or attention, gave Kate a loud snort as she turned to leave the barn. It was kind of a condensed "come back when you can't stay so long" sarcastic snip, in horse language. The gesture was, unfortunately, moot due to the simultaneous loud squeak from the closing of the large front door of the barn.

No one has ever clearly identified the thinking capacity of which an animal is capable, but it's not entirely unlikely that Sanchez, while standing in that stall nursing his oat rations on this particular morning, may have been reminiscing about the time he left Kate up in that meadow to walk home on her own, because he was definitely sporting a look that could easily have been mistaken for a grin when the door closed.

At 10:00 Kate was sitting at the kitchen table waiting for her dad to get off the phone. That's what he did with most of his day. His job required him to do a lot of phone work from home. When he came walking out of his office, she thought she noticed a less cheerful look on his face than earlier. Her immediate thought was that she needed a parent in a cooperative mood at this meeting. On the way out the door, she gave a quick turn, thinking about grabbing the "Annie" tape for the ride into town, anything to ensure that his mood was conducive to agreeing with her strategy of fending off all possible alternatives to this summer school idea. She decided against it. He knew she was less than fond of his music, and it would have been too obvious if she brought it along.

As it turned out, the ride to school was pretty silent. Somewhere along the way, Kate figured out that it wasn't a bad mood kind of silence, but more the 'caught up in work' type, which came as a relief.

On the way down the hall to the Principal's office, they passed several classrooms in session. Looking in through the door glass as she passed, and seeing the blank stares on the pained faces of kids so obviously wishing they were somewhere else, Kate immediately felt the added anxiety. What if this doesn't go her way, and she ends up in one of these rooms next week? She suddenly wished she hadn't eaten.

It was then and there, just as she stepped into the Principal's outer office where Mrs. Elliott usually sits, that she decided to take a stand. If there was an alternate class offered, she was going to look her dad in the eye and tell him she could not bear the idea, that she had agreed to this solely to please him, and that she would take her chances on college with her grades as they stood. Sort of an "if a college isn't interested in me, the way I am, then I'm not interested in them" angle.

"Ah, hello there Kate," beamed Mr. Breen as he came walking out of his office. "And you must be Mr. Bennett," he said as he shook her father's hand. "Thanks so much for coming down. Why don't we go into my office?"

When Mr. Breen got to his desk, he picked up a folder from the pile on his desk, opened it and studied it for a few seconds.

"I'm sure your dad has told you, Kate, that Mr. Talbot has canceled his summer science course. I wanted you both to come in today because I don't have an easy answer to satisfy your request to get this make up grade in before the school year begins."

Mr. Breen went on to explain that the other six students signed up for this class had opted to take a Saturday morning session with Mr. Talbot during the first semester of the coming school year. When he asked Kate if she would be interested in the same alternative, she was quick to point out that there were two key horse competitions that would take place on Saturdays in the fall, without actually mentioning the fact that she had no real intention of entering either, and asked about the *other* possible choices.

"Well," said Mr. Breen after a long pause, "I'm afraid that's the only *structured* course the school can offer at this time. Of course, you could always consider an accredited tutor. But, that is typically an expensive proposition."

"Is there someone available?" asked her dad.

"As a matter of fact, in preparation for this meeting, I checked the only two certified teachers at this school to see if one of them might be convinced to take on this kind of an assignment on such short notice. To my surprise Ms. Turner told me that she would consider it."

"Ms. *Jaycee* Turner? The *French* teacher?" a confused Kate blurted out.

"Yes, actually, the French teacher." he replied. "You see, Ms. Turner was originally certified in Natural Sciences at the secondary level, and later became certified in French as well. When she moved here we were looking for a French teacher, and she was happy with either, although I have the feeling that science would have been her first choice. There hasn't been any doubt in my mind during her short time here that Roosevelt High is very lucky to have her. She is certainly a very talented teacher, and extremely good with the students."

Mr. Breen then went on to tell them that they should contact Ms. Turner directly if they were interested in pursuing this.

He gave the phone number to Kate's dad, and reminded him that, although any expenses incurred could not be the responsibility of the school, he would personally coordinate the requirements of the program with Ms. Turner, and offer any materials she might need to teach the course, if she decided to do it. With that, and a courteous thanks and goodbye from all parties, the meeting was over and Kate and her dad were on their way back to the car.

Kate was positively beaming. Without having to face the embarrassment of taking the stand that she had intended, it seemed as though things were working out pretty well. If Jaycee Turner decided not to accept the job of tutoring, it looked pretty certain that there would be no more options to consider, so the case would be closed. On the other hand, if she *did* accept the job, well, Kate loved Ms. Turner as a teacher. She had just told Mallory yesterday that she loved French because Ms. Turner was the best teacher she ever had, and that it was a shame there weren't more teachers like her at Roosevelt.

The 'Big Sky Grill' was Kate's choice when her dad asked where they should have lunch. There was no place Kate knew of that could match the onion rings they served. They were huge. It was just an ordinary sort of roadside place, but it was always crowded. Lots of people from town ate there regularly, along with the new faces of people headed up or down the interstate. It was only a mile and a half off the highway, and had a reputation for being well worth the few extra minutes it took to get there.

This was only the third time Kate and her father had been to the Big Sky Grill all summer. Ms. Turner later told them that she came here every Wednesday for lunch because it was conveniently on the way to some committee meeting she attended each week, and because of the onion rings. How it happened that she showed up there at *this* lunch hour, on *this* day, as they were just returning from the school with *her* phone number to call, well, that's clearly one of those really unexplainable coincidences.

"Ms. Turner?" an awestruck Kate called out as they walked into the Big Sky Grill. She spotted her teacher in the very front booth as they were walking to their table.

"Well, hey Kate. Comment Allez Vous?" Ms. Turner said as she looked up from the book she was reading.

Kate was way too dumbfounded to answer in French. Even the English she attempted could have used some light translation.

"It's , uh, I'm ….good, …good. Jeez, what are you doing here?"

"What my smooth talking daughter means is that it is a real coincidence to see you here. We were just coming from a meeting with Mr. Breen and you were part of the discussion. He told us that you might be interested in tutoring Kate in science these next few weeks, and, oh, I'm very sorry, I'm Michael Bennett, but please, we don't mean to interrupt your lunch. Perhaps we should give you a call about this later."

"It's nice to meet you Mr. Bennett. I'm Jaycee Turner. And please, why don't you both sit down and join me here. I haven't ordered yet, so we can discuss this whole thing over lunch if you wish."

The next thing Kate knew, she was taking the inside position in the booth, still at a loss for words. She hadn't even had time to give the tutoring idea any real thought. At first, it sounded great. She wouldn't be stuck in that school building staring out the window every morning, and she liked the idea of having Ms. Turner as a tutor. But the whole concept was still too new to have given it enough consideration to be anything but neutral at this point. She had convinced herself, after all, that she was not going to make up the class at all.

"Mr. Breen explained your intent to make up the last semester grade in order to make a better looking transcript for college, Kate, and I must say, I think that's a very mature decision on your part."

"Ms. Turner," Kate's father began.

"Please call me Jaycee, Mr. Bennett."

"Very well. Jaycee, have you given the idea of tutoring Kate any further thought? That is any more thought since you spoke to Mr. Breen? He seemed to indicate that you *might* consider it."

"Yes, I have, Mr. Bennett, I…"

"Please, I can't call you Jaycee, if you still call me Mr. Bennett. It's Michael."

"Fair enough. Yes, I have, Michael. My problem is that, unfortunately, I don't think it's possible with what little free time I have over these next few weeks."

"Does that mean you can't do it, Ms. Turner?" asked Kate.

"Well, what it means is that I couldn't do it in the traditional sense, with a regular set schedule. But, if you were willing to work with me a few nights during the next two weeks, and at least a couple of Saturdays in September I believe we could get the necessary work done in time for the deadline to get your grade changed.

"I would have to get Mr. Breen's approval, but as long as we can keep track of the hours, meet for the required amount of time and turn in the proper assignments, I don't see why he would object."

"How long each Saturday?" Kate posed, as delicately and politely as possible.

"Don't worry, Kate, I won't make you spend any more of your free time than absolutely required. But, just so you understand, eighteen hours class time, plus assignments, is the minimum. If we can get three or four full classes in before school starts, we should only need two or three Saturdays, a few hours each."

"I'd be willing to do that, I guess," offered Kate. "But where?"

"I think it would be easiest if we met at my house. But, if you have trouble getting rides I will gladly come and get you, or drop you off afterward. Where do you live by the way?"

"We live out by the Rota farm. It's really easy place to find." she replied. "It's the only house on Redstone Hill Road with a horse barn."

"I don't think there will be much of a problem getting her back and forth to your house, Jaycee," added her dad. "My schedule has been pretty flexible lately. Do you live in town?"

"Yes, I'm not far from the school actually, on Dearborn Road."

"I guess that only leaves the matter of compensation. Mr. Breen didn't really give me any indication about what the cost of this would be," Kate's father said, sheepishly.

"I don't want to alarm you, but this would be my first tutoring job in years, and the first one since I've been out here," Jaycee Turner admitted. "So, I don't really even know what the going rate is now. But, since you're going to do it around my schedule, I really don't even feel that I need to take any money for it."

"Well, I couldn't allow that, and I'm very sorry if I made you feel uncomfortable asking about it. Believe me, I'm sure Kate is thrilled at the prospect of not having to go to that school building every morning for this course. And I know she was dreading the fact that she was going to have to take it with Mr. Talbot again, so please, we want to make sure that you are fairly compensated for your time. Right Kate?"

Just as he finished saying it, the waitress put his B.L.T. in front of him. She had served the ladies just a few seconds before, which caused Kate to shift her attention to the pile of golden brown onion rings right in front of her face.

"Right Kate?" her dad asked again.

"I'm sorry, Dad, I missed that. Right what?"

"It doesn't matter, sweetheart, I'm sure that you agree, and I should have known better than to disturb you once those rings were served anyway," her dad said with a smile.

Jaycee looked like she was deep in thought. "You know," she said. "I just had an idea." She sipped her iced tea and looked at Kate. "Might you be interested in bartering for these tutoring sessions?"

Looking less than 100% confident she understood, "That's trading, right?" Kate asked.

"Yes. Trading. I remember you telling me last semester that you gave riding lessons. How would you feel about giving me lessons in exchange for the tutoring?" she proposed in a somewhat excited manner.

"Well, sure," Kate replied. "Have you ridden at all?"

"No, not since I was very young. But, I have wanted to learn for many years now and, who knows, maybe one day have a horse of my own."

"Kate is a very experienced rider," boasted her dad, "and I'm sure she could get you pretty well into the intermediate stage of riding ability. But, I don't think that riding lessons command the same kind of dollars that tutoring does."

"It would be a very fair deal for me, Michael. I'm kind of excited that this will force me to finally do it. What do you say, Kate, do we have a deal?"

"Deal!" said Kate, smiling as she accepted Jaycee's outstretched hand to confirm the agreement.

Through the rest of lunch each discussed what the other would need for the respective lessons. Jaycee said she would get the textbook from school, and Kate offered to provide a riding helmet if she wanted one, though she told her that she was sure a good old western hat would feel more appropriate.

By the end of lunch, the first class was set for the following evening at Jaycee's house. Michael insisted on paying for lunch, both because he appreciated the amazing coincidence that they ran into Jaycee on this particular day, and because he said he came out way ahead on the deal since he was obviously expecting to pay for the tutoring.

Star of night, distant light,
from candles on night's ceiling.
Suns of old, some gone cold,
do dwarf this lonely feeling.

Chapter Two

Astronomy

On the way up Redstone Hill, Kate was thinking that, rather than dreading this extra schoolwork she found herself feeling very positive about this first session with Ms. Turner. She looked forward to finding out more about her. There was something about her that made her seem quite different from the other women teachers, and different from most of the 'older' women Kate knew. It was apparent in the way she carried herself, and in the way she was able to attract attention without effort. Even the school showoffs rarely got out of line in her class. Of course, these same goofs never fooled around in gym class either, because they knew Mr. Herbst would humiliate them publicly by inviting them to assist him with some sort of physical demonstration on "Judo, the art of self defense." But, with Ms. Turner, it seemed that it was more out of respect than fear.

Jaycee Turner had only moved to town a bit more than a year prior, and in that time no one that Kate knew really ever said much about her. By any comparison, she would be considered a very attractive woman, and it was known that she lived alone, yet no one ever talked about her dating. Of course, it could happen that she was seeing someone from out of town on occasion and was discreet enough that nobody knew. But, although people like Mal's parents had nothing but praise for her personal demeanor, and at school she was probably the favorite teacher of the majority of students, there was still an intriguing sort of mystery about her. She wasn't from the area, and that was usually enough to create some amount of suspicion in these parts.

The two hours absolutely whisked by that evening. The concept of latent energy was not nearly as boring as it was during the school year. Actually, Kate only vaguely remembered ever having covered this particular part of the subject matter in Mr. Talbot's class. She imagined that it may well have come up during one of those classes she slept through.

Truly, presentation *is* the thing. There was no question in Kate's mind as she left that evening that she was not only able to begin to grasp the concept of energy but, incredibly, she even found it interesting. Ms. Turner had a way, just as she did in French class, of making the subject matter relate to everyday life. By the end of the two hours, she and Kate were having a discussion about science as if it might have occurred by chance, just as she and Mallory would discuss music, or boys.

When her dad came to pick her up, he came to the door and rang the bell. Until that point, there was no mention of when the next session would be. As Kate gathered her papers and shoved them in her notebook, Ms. Turner said "Tell your dad that I will pick you up for the next session, so he doesn't have to come all the way over here twice in an evening. And don't forget to read the next chapter!" she called out as Kate was about to leave.

"When will that be?" asked Kate.

"Actually, tomorrow would be good for me. Do you think you could make it tomorrow, maybe around the same time?"

"Fine for me," Kate answered as she opened the door. "All set Dad," she said as she stepped out onto the porch. "Goodnight, Ms. Turner," she yelled back through the screen.

"Goodnight Kate," echoed from inside.

That evening, just before going to bed, Kate looked at the chapter she was supposed to read. "Thirty pages to read for tomorrow," she sulked.

On Thursday morning, it was pretty apparent that the weather was changing for the better. For the past several days, it had been quite warm for this area, with very little air movement of any kind, but on this morning there was already a cool breeze fanning the curtains in Kate's room when she woke up. The part of the sky that she could see from her bed was lit up in orange across the horizon. It was a classic western sunrise. "This could be a good day to ride up to the meadow to do that reading," she thought to herself as she sat up in bed. "It is, after all, a 'St. Cloud' day," she said out loud as she stared at the art print directly in front of her.

On opposite walls in Kate's room, hung two prints she had bought in a quaint little art studio in Santa Fe during the prior summer. She spent close to three weeks wages on them but, as happens with the instant appeal of any work of art, she was immediately captivated when she eyed "The Scream" in the shop window for the first time, and the subsequent hour of looking at more and more options at several other stores did little to diminish the temptation.

Returning to the gallery to find out the cost of the item she just had to have, she was shown another Munch print, "Night in St. Cloud", as a slightly less expensive option.

It was another instant connection and, in Kate's words, an "emotion provoking" work that created quite a dilemma. Which to buy?

The idea that Kate would be so drawn to works of art would not even mildly surprise anyone that knew her, but to have found something worthy of adorning her notoriously bare walls was another matter altogether. Unlike most girls her age, there had never been posters of rock bands, teen idols or movie stars in her room. As much as she appreciated some of those she had seen at friend's houses, she never really found one that struck her as something she needed to see on a daily basis.

With only a few minutes of deliberation, Kate decided to buy both prints that day, as these were works she felt she definitely could, and would, look at everyday.

It was easy to relate to "The Scream". Even teenage girls without an appreciation for art could find the frustration and fear that this artist conveyed somewhat familiar in such an 'I'm not pretty enough', 'I don't fit in', 'he doesn't like me' world. Kate's instant attraction to "Night in St. Cloud", though, stemmed from what she would later explain as "layers of incredible strokes that draw the viewer into the scene in order to examine the man that sits, so alone, looking out a window."

When Kate woke up on her left side, as she did this day, she would be facing the 'St. Cloud' print, and at some point during her junior year, she had begun to notice that the 'St. Cloud' days seemed to somehow turn out better than those which began with a view of "The Scream". Of course, this was based less on fact than a general retrospective of highlights associated with either, so as much as the 'St. Cloud' days may have been cause for a more positive outlook early on in the day, "The Scream" may well have influenced the judgment, maybe even subconsciously, in just the opposite way.

The importance of hope, though, might best be noted by the fact that the normal preference to sleeping on her back for most of her young life had gradually given way to a tendency toward the left-side sometime *after* the posters were hung.

After tending to the horses and cleaning up the breakfast dishes, Kate put together a quick lunch, saddled Sanchez, wrote a note to her father in case he came back early and headed out to enjoy the day, homework and all.

After ten pages of reading, she realized that she wasn't really remembering much of what she read. It definitely wasn't as interesting as Ms. Turner had made it during the first session, so taking an early lunch break seemed to be the timely thing to do. Of course, when Sanchez heard the sandwich coming out of the wrapper, he hopped his way back over next to Kate in case there was something packed for him. Kate took some apple slices out of her bag and let him take one at a time out of the palm of her hand while she updated him on what she had read. This was something she tended to do before tests, as she was convinced verbalizing what was read helped her to remember it. Sanchez always seemed grateful for the education, perhaps realizing it was rare among his kind, so he was always a good listener. On this day, though, as soon as he was convinced that there was no more apple to be had, he began to hop back over to the tall grass, leaving Kate talking to herself with her eyes closed.

"Maybe a short rest is in order before tackling the second half of this chapter," she thought. She resealed the bag and set it back on the log behind her, eased back on the blanket and rested her head on the book. The thought of absorbing some of the knowledge from the book through osmosis while she slept occurred to her as she closed her eyes, but the sound of the slight breeze rustling the grass around her put her to sleep before she could give the matter much consideration.

Sometime between the thought of absorbing the knowledge and the moment of waking, Sanchez had made his way back to the blanket. He brought her out of a sound sleep with a snort. She resisted opening her eyes until he finally put his head close enough that she could feel the breath coming from his nostrils.

"What time is it, boy?" she asked, eyes still closed.

Sanchez just pulled his head back and snorted again to let her know that he was finished with grazing. Even with his education, his internal clock was capable of discerning only two times of the day, mealtime, and not mealtime, so the question was answered as far as he was concerned.

When she looked at her watch, she realized that she had slept for more than an hour, and even in that groggy condition, she figured out that by the time she got back and finished her chores there would be very little time to read the rest of the assignment before getting dinner ready. She and her dad had a system of taking turns preparing and cleaning up after dinner, and this was her night. So she slowly pulled herself up, folded the blanket, stuck it in the saddlebag along with the book, and took the cuffs off of Sanchez. Still less than 100% awake, she hadn't noticed that Sanchez had knocked the lunch bag off, and behind, the log on which it was sitting.

Somewhere about two thirds of the way back, Kate remembered that she did not collect it in her hasty departure. Since it belonged to her dad and it was one of those fairly new kind of zippered insulated bags, she contemplated going back for it, but, she knew that by the time she got back and got Sanchez put away it would really be getting late to get everything done, and since no one else ever went up there anyway, she decided it would be okay to wait until the next day to get it. That way, there would still be time to get to the last few pages of reading, even with the sort of slow paced dinner her dad preferred more often than not, as she wasn't going to be picked up for a few of hours yet.

The sound of the oven timer signaled the completion of the heating cycle for the previously frozen chicken potpie, and the end of the allotted reading time. Kate closed the book, with only two pages left to read, called her dad in from his office and put the iced tea and pot pie on the table next to the fresh bread he had brought home with him.

The conversation during dinner mainly involved a potential trip to Albuquerque over the weekend to look at a horse that was offered to Kate's dad for free. He had done some work for the people who owned the horse and they contacted him to find out if he would be interested in taking it. They were moving back east and felt strongly about finding a good home for the animal rather than selling it.

"What do you think, Kate?" asked her father. "Do we need another mouth to feed? As I recall, it is a beautiful quarter horse," he reflected as he put some of the pot pie in his plate. "Though I have no idea what she's like. I only caught a brief glimpse of her once when I was down there."

"Well, if we don't keep her, I know Ms. Turner said she would be looking for a horse as soon as she feels comfortable about riding," Kate replied.

"You know," he noted after thinking for a moment, "that's not a bad idea at all. Since she would probably board her here, it would mean a bit of extra income for you instead of another expense for me. What do you say we go down and have a look this weekend?"

"Sure Dad, but I have to ask a favor of you right now. Ms. Turner is due to pick me up any minute now, so I won't have time to clean up here. Do you suppose we could swap nights and I'll clean up after dinner for you tomorrow night?"

"No problem, sweetheart. I almost forgot you had a class this evening. I need to find out what time to pick you up later. Will you ask Jaycee and let me know before you leave?"

Kate nodded as she walked out onto the porch. While she waited, she opened the book to get some last minute reading in since she didn't see the car down the long driveway yet. A few minutes later when Sam, the elderly household guard dog, barked, Kate looked up and saw Ms. Turner's car coming. Within two seconds, the second alarm of the estate was sounded. Sanchez had his head sticking out the upper door to his stall and was voicing his dislike for strangers.

After a calm assurance to Sam, who these days was clearly more content with warning the family about potential breaches of security than actually getting up and investigating them, and a yell to Sanchez that everything was okay, she closed the book and got up to greet her tutor. Even though she was able to complete the reading assignment, Kate was still a bit nervous about the fact that she really couldn't remember much of it.

Her dad was standing at the front door when she got in the car, and before she could even ask about the time he needed to pick her up, Ms. Turner stepped out of her side of the car and shouted "How are you, Michael?"

"Fine thank you, Jaycee, and how are you this evening?" he answered through the screen.

"Good too, thanks. We'll be finishing a little later tonight, maybe around 10:00, so there is no need for you to pick up Kate. I'll bring her home."

"That's not at all necessary, Jaycee. I don't want you going out of your way. You are already doing us a great favor by spending your spare time tutoring Kate. I sure don't expect transportation as part of the deal."

By the time he said it she was already back in the car and yelled out through the window next to Kate, "Actually we are going on a field trip this evening not far from here, so it will be just as easy for me to drive back by here. Really, it's not an inconvenience at all," Ms. Turner assured him.

"Okay, if you say so. Then I'll see you around ten, Kate." As he finished speaking, the car was already in motion. He didn't hear Kate's goodbye over the sound of the wheels on the gravel, but he saw her wave from the window as they headed back down the driveway.

"Well, Kate," Ms. Turner said as she turned the car onto the paved road, "just before I left my house this evening I decided that it would be a perfect night to cover the astronomy introduction which normally comes at the end of the course. I think we will be able to see a good deal of what we need to see tonight because there is only a sliver of a moon, and the cooler weather today has cleared the sky of all that haze that's been around the past few days."

"I don't remember covering any astronomy last year, Ms. Turner."

"That's really a shame, but it is somewhat typical in this course. A shame in my opinion, but typical. Because there's *so* much to cover in this course the astronomy intro is usually sacrificed to allow enough time for the more basic stuff. But, since it happens to be my favorite part of the course, I always found a way to get this section in early when I taught science. So, tonight it will be my intention to open your mind to the wonder of the night sky. What do you think?"

"Sounds good to me, but what about the reading?" Kate asked.

"Not to worry, young study, we will get back to the more mundane material next session, so your reading time will by no means have been wasted. But, for now, come outside and let's observe the heavens."

At that moment, the car was pulled to a stop on the side of an old deserted trail that, at one time, led to a pretty popular fishing spot. But, once the dam was completed up river the small lake dried up and no one ever really used it anymore. Kate was familiar with the old road because she had ridden out this way a few times on horseback.

As the lights were turned off, and they closed the car doors behind them, it was so dark that Kate had to feel her way along to get to the front of the car.

"You see, Kate, this cannot be appreciated in the classroom. God! It's like a Van Gogh painting out here tonight," Ms. Turner said with genuine excitement in her voice. "How could one do justice describing Van Gogh's 'Starry Night'?" Ms. Turner asked.

"I come out here, on occasion, and sit for hours with my telescope, looking at one thing or another. When there is minimal moonlight, like tonight, the sky is literally aglow with visible stars. Just look at that!" Ms. Turner said as she pointed toward the sky.

It *was* a perfect night for this sort of thing, thought Kate. She was not unfamiliar with stargazing. Her father had owned a telescope when she was younger, and had introduced her to some of the basic stars and all of the planets. She remembered her father had spent many a night out on the porch with that telescope. But, he sold it at a flea market a few years back, and she was wondering just *why* he had gotten rid of it when he seemed to have enjoyed it so much.

"Kate?"

"Yes, Ma'am?"

"I thought you drifted off on me there. Please spare my feelings and tell me I'm not boring you. I was just pointing out the Leo constellation and I couldn't help but notice you weren't looking," Ms. Turner stated with a smile.

"I'm really sorry, Ms. Turner. I was just having a flashback of doing this kind of thing when I was little, with my dad. No, honestly, this isn't the least bit boring. I'm sorry."

"Your dad was a stargazer?" she asked.

"Yes, when my mother was alive he spent a lot of time out on the porch with his telescope, sometimes with me on his lap, just looking out there. I haven't thought about that in a long time, and I was just wondering why he got rid of that old telescope."

"Maybe there wasn't the time anymore," Jaycee suggested as she gazed at the sky.

"Yeah, I'm sure that was probably it. I was just thinking that there were probably a lot of other things he had to give up for my sake," Kate reflected.

"Hold on there, Kate!" Ms. Turner jumped in. "If it is of any consolation, quite honestly, I got the feeling that your father was a very happy man when I met him. Believe me, that's a quality that I always thought was pretty easy to spot in a person. Lots of people walk around with that beaten look in their eyes, wearing their bad breaks like heavy weights on their shoulders, as though they are hoping to be asked just how bad things have been for them. Others, though, have that look like they have been trusted with some big secret about how everything is going to turn out. Your father definitely looks like he's more in *that* group.

"Anyway, we have got to get back to science. I was about to tell you about Carl Sagan, one of the really intriguing speakers on this subject today. He wrote about the earth being a 'cosmic shore', so I would like to try this little experiment if you can give me your complete attention for just a moment. What I would like you to do is to get totally relaxed, and close your eyes for a minute or two. Just try to use all of your brain to focus on what I tell you for a few minutes."

As Kate leaned back against the hood of the car and closed her eyes, Jaycee continued; "First, just try to imagine life a very long time ago, back when people hunted for food. Try to conjure up your own picture of early man. Take a minute to do that.

"Then, let's have this person standing at the shoreline of the ocean, his knowledge of what the rest of the world looked like limited by the horizon.

"Now, this being that you have pictured, probably has the brain matter necessary to wonder what might be beyond this natural boundary. Eventually, that wonder would motivate him to figure out a way to fashion a small craft and venture out onto the water. As his curiosity grows, and his understanding of sea-going vessels expands, he would learn to journey further and further out until, finally, the barrier is overcome, and the ocean is crossed.

"Mr. Sagan's reference to the whole earth being a 'cosmic shore' puts us in the same curious position as early man at the ocean's edge. It's just a different boundary. These days we find ourselves looking out into space and wondering what might be out *there*. And, so far, you can see we have fashioned some very crude spacecraft to go out relatively short distances to explore. But, we obviously haven't scratched the surface of what we need to understand about the physics necessary to accomplish much greater journeys. With what we know, moving through space to places we can see through a telescope would take several lifetimes, so we are still the 'early man', so to speak, at *this* shore."

When Kate opened her eyes again, there seemed to be even more stars visible than a few seconds before when she closed them. In that short span of time, not only did the stars multiply, but her impression of the size of the universe did as well, and her appreciation for how much of it mankind was capable of knowing was reduced considerably, forever.

After pointing out the shape of Leo, and showing Kate how to find it by using the 'pointing' stars of the Big Dipper in reverse, Ms. Turner gave her a tour of the most visible stars, and with her binoculars she was able to show the life stages of a star. Blue for new, red for old. "Unfortunately, I can't show you my favorite star. It won't be rising until very late," she said. "but I'm sure you are familiar with the 'dog star', Sirius, right Kate?"

"That's the really bright one, isn't it?" she asked.

"Very good! It is, indeed, the brightest star visible to us. Any idea why it came to be known as the dog star?"

"Uh, no. I guess not," Kate confessed.

"Well, it's part of the constellation Canis Major, or 'great dog'. Orion's faithful companion. As a matter of fact, the term 'dog days' of summer comes from that time of year when the dog star rises with the sun. What *I* happen to find most intriguing about this star, though, is that it is a double star, or *twin* star. It shares its existence with another star. And because this other star never blocks the light of Sirius from our view, this fact wasn't even known until just about 100 years ago. The twin is a dying star in its last stage of life, burning white hot, so I can't help but wonder what will happen to Sirius as the other dies off. I remember my high school science teacher referring to the whole scenario as this "celestial opera." He said it was because the sad scenario of this brilliant star, slowly losing its lifelong mate, was being played out in the sky, for all to see. Something of a 'Madama Butterfly' in the heavens he used to say."

"Is Sirius so bright because it's closest to us?" Kate wondered.

"That's a good question!" complimented Jaycee. "But no, although it is close in *relative* terms, a mere nine light years away, there are actually several stars closer to us. Brightness, you need to understand, has to do with both distance *and* size. It is the combination of size and proximity, or - large enough *and* close enough – that makes Sirius so bright in our sky.

"Another one of the interesting descriptions I remember, one related to brightness and distance of stars anyway, is the fact that in some cases we are looking at ghost stars out there."

"Ghosts?"

"Well, depending on how far away the star, we wouldn't know it had died, or collapsed, for a number of years after it actually happened, as light generated years prior would still be on its way to us. So, occasionally, the twinkling we see is actually something of a ghost light from a star that no longer exists".

"Really strange to think of it that way." Kate acknowledged.

As they got back into the car to leave that night Kate realized that she had become familiar with more than she ever thought she would like to know about the night sky, and that Ms. Turner was absolutely right. This could never have been appreciated in the same way being taught from a textbook in a classroom. On the way back home, Kate planned to ask her dad why he got rid of the telescope, and whether he would consider getting another.

"One flesh; to lose thee were to lose myself"

Milton

Chapter Three

Psychology

Just about sixteen months prior to Jaycee's impromptu meeting with Kate and her father at the "Big Sky", she stood on the porch of her parent's house on a cold March New England evening, and cried as she contemplated the incredible life change she was about to undertake.

She slipped out to the porch when she felt she could no longer control her emotions, and stood there listening to the dozen or so voices on the other side of the window, all of whom came to say their goodbyes.

This was to be the last night among friends, family and familiar surroundings before beginning her cross-country drive to her new home in New Mexico, and as much as the idea of starting anew, in a place where she knew absolutely no-one, was at times more than she could think about, it seemed more and more a worthwhile experiment in putting her life back in order as time went on.

Sitting on the porch stairs, the sound of a car turning the corner and crunching the residual sand and salt left on the road, the typical sound on any city street at the end of a long New England winter, triggered a memory of the nights that she and her sister would play cards until dark on that porch, with that unmistakable sound in the background.

Her father came out to sit next to her on the stairs. He put his arm around her, and assured her that no one would be missing her more than he.

"I've come 180 degrees though," he admitted, struggling to contain his emotion.

"I sincerely believe that it *is* the right course of action for you at this point, and I know it will put you back in the game of living".

With eyes welling, he told her that he was absolutely prepared to "pull up stakes" and move west with her if she felt she needed the company and support, but was convinced that her new beginning would require independence.

Jaycee wasn't completely surprised by the sentiment, that he would leave the place he had lived his entire life to follow her if she needed him, because she had always felt that he would make any sacrifice necessary to make she and her sister happy, but the emotions were already raw and the realization that he would not be nearby after tomorrow was suddenly overwhelming. They had spent a lot of time together since she moved home, and he had been a huge factor in her healing process.

To heal, Webster would contend, is to restore health, wellness or soundness. In Jaycee's case, the process was understandably, painstakingly slow, and although the long term outlook was not to be as well, as sound or by any means as happy as the days before her son disappeared, she had worked her way back to a point that she felt healthy and able to fend off the once debilitating depression that comes with such a tragic loss.

Timothy was not only the light of his mother's life, but as the first grandchild for her parents, and the first nephew for her sister, he was the light of many lives from the moment he was born. He was given the name Timothy after her father, and his middle name, Jackson, came from her husband's dad, who had died a few years before her and her husband had met.

Jaycee met her former husband at a farm store, where both were ordering pies just prior to Thanksgiving, while in her senior year at Clark University. Bill had finished law school and was waiting for the results of his bar exam. He struck up a conversation as they stood there enjoying some coffee and the incredible scent of fresh baked apple pies cooling on the counter.

While she was aware even at that point that, by all measures, he did not fit the profile of what most would qualify as 'her type', there was a mysterious, worldly intellectual quality about him that she immediately found at least intriguing.

Easy to second guess later, but by the time she was beginning her first year in grad school, she was returning from a four day honeymoon on Cape Cod, which was all the time either could spare, since Bill had landed a job with the federal government as a liaison to the FBI witness protection program, and was to report the day after Labor day. It was a prestigious job for a lawyer right out of school, but he scored very well on the bar, and had a bit of an in with one of the senior agents in the Boston district who he had met during one of his night classes at New England School of Law.

There were problems with the relationship early on, mostly having to do with Bill showing a controlling side that hadn't been at all visible during the dating process, but much was ignored or attributed to a very hectic and trying schedule for both. By the end of Jaycee's first year of graduate school, she was pregnant, and as much as Bill seemed less enthusiastic than her about the prospect of having a child, he did come around when Timothy was born the following spring. By that time, though, his job was beginning to require some extensive travel back and forth to Washington, and Bill hated the fact that he was missing precious time with his new son during his first year.

It wasn't long before Bill was consumed by the job, and it became clear that it was only his son that caused him to return home as often as possible. The relationship between he and Jaycee had deteriorated to the point that when he did spend nights at home, he took up residence in the guest room.

This was not the way Jaycee had envisioned married life. She had completed her graduate studies, thanks in no small way to her parents caring for her boy during the day, but had not looked for a teaching position for the two years following. Bill had insisted that he did not want a nanny, or anyone else taking care of his son, and that he could make enough money for them to make ends meet. His promise was that once the boy entered school, it would be an "appropriate" time for her to seek a job in her chosen profession. Even then, he often cited, it was only agreeable because a teaching job would obviously coincide with the school hours for their son, and a babysitter would not be required.

By the time Timothy, TJ as she came to call him, was a bit more than three, Jaycee decided to accept a teaching position and, in doing so, knew she would need to separate herself from Bill in order to lead a normal life.

To say that the divorce bombshell was not taken well would almost be overstating it.

Bill was surprisingly calm after hearing of Jaycee's request. But, to *her* surprise, his interpretation was that she was leaving to begin a life of her own, which didn't become clear until Bill admitted that he was completely prepared to live without her, but hoped that she felt "responsible" enough to wait until he could find a proper person to care for their son while he was working.

When she made it clear that there was no way she was leaving Timothy, and Bill understood that it was he who was going to leave the family, at her bequest, he did come a bit unglued, and did actually say that he would rather see her dead before that would ever happen. It was this statement, an obvious 'faux pas' from one with such an education in the law, that eventually resulted in a restraining order, and from that night forward they would never again speak to one another face to face.

During the ensuing year, and through a costly divorce process, custody of Timothy was always the issue, and while Jaycee always harbored a degree of fear that Bill could pull off a miracle and obtain custody, she remained mostly confident that there was no possibility for him to portray her as an unfit mother. It did, however, become painfully clear that he was willing to use any means at his disposal to win when he presented to the judge an affidavit from a woman Jaycee never met, who swore that she was with Jaycee when they consumed cocaine together at a sorority function during her last year at grad school.

Fortunately, the alleged incident came at a time when Jaycee was experiencing a bout of 'post partum' thyroid problems, and was seeing her family doctor regularly. A chart of monthly blood screening results was presented as proof that there were no traces of illegal substances found in her system during that period of time, and the judge strongly cautioned Bill and his counsel about the possibility of a separate 'criminal' process if it was ever proven that such an affidavit was either not authentic or "ill conspired".

In the end, Bill was given fairly liberal, unsupervised visitation rights, though there were to be no sleepover visits until the court reviewed the matter after one year under the present agreement.

It was agreed, over the phone, that visitations would take place on Sundays, and in order to conform to the still in existence restraining order, Bill would pick up and drop off Timothy at Jaycee's sister's house, and this went surprisingly well for 21 Sundays in a row.

When it came to TJ's fourth birthday, which landed on a Saturday, Bill made a special request to trade his Sunday for Saturday that weekend, so that he could spend some time with him on his special day, have him open a few presents and do something fun, and promised that he would still have him back in time for dinner.

Jaycee and her parents decided they could get together and celebrate her son's birthday at dinner that evening, so Jaycee felt that she was to some degree extending a deserved kindness to Bill, who she couldn't help but feel sympathy for through the whole process, and agreed to the change.

Jaycee's sister was to drive TJ directly to her parent's house for dinner and a small party. The dining room table was decorated for the occasion, and the presents were stacked on the hutch, but when it got to be 7:30, an hour after Bill promised to drop off his son, Jaycee had already made two calls to her sister, one to Bill's apartment and one to his office. The next call, at 8:55, was to the police. By this time, of course, the family was moderately concerned, but not in any sort of panic, as it could happen that whatever birthday plan Bill had may have gone over, and he may have lost track of time. The idea that it could be car trouble, though, soon turned to fear of an accident, but the possibility that Bill would actually kidnap his own son was not considered until the police reported that they have been in contact with his employer, and that he had taken an extended leave of absence.

Although Jaycee had several phone conversations with Bill, she hadn't actually seen him since the courtroom, and the morning of TJ's fourth birthday, when she dropped him off at her sister's, kissed him goodbye and told him to "have a great birthday with dad" was the last time she saw her son.

In the early days of the ordeal, there was disbelief, and an assumption that the nightmare would end when they were found, and even some advance thought given to an end of any visitations in the future. As days turned to weeks, though, and the FBI found that Bill had apparently planned the escape with all the expertise he accumulated in his dealings with relocating people and creating new identities for them, the possibility that this would, at the very least, be a long process was setting in.

After six weeks of following dead end leads, one well meaning agent told her that there may not be a person in the country more prepared to disappear, and that would include CIA agents.

At 10 weeks, with the help of her father she hired a private investigator that specialized in finding fugitives from justice. He provided a new spark of confidence, as he predicted that he could find anyone, and that no one can disappear, especially with a child in tow.

When the private investigation consumed twenty thousand dollars in fees, Jaycee's dad offered to take out a second mortgage on his house, but the investigator said he would put his own time into the case, and worked another six weeks beyond the original commitment before telling them that, in all likelihood, her former husband had probably taken up residence in another country, where it would be almost impossible to track him down.

This made some sense, as a set of cassette tapes for learning French was among the things found in Bill's apartment when they searched, but there was speculation that this might be left just to throw them off the trail, because it would seem like one of the things a person would want to bring along if they were moving to a French speaking country.

Six months passed quickly. With all the things that were involved in finding TJ, there was plenty of time for second-guessing, and self-blame for not anticipating such a thing, but not a lot of time given to the possibility of this being a permanent loss.

The horror of losing a child, Jaycee was learning, comes in facing the finality of not being with them ever again. As this possibility began to work its way into Jaycee's prospects, she attempted to keep the grief at bay by conducting her own investigation, calling every clinic and local medical bureau she could research to find out if a four year old boy matching TJ's description had been brought in by his father for a preschool sort of health screening or shots of any kind. This investigation even involved the province of Quebec for a couple of weeks, as it seemed a likely place to hide for someone that could speak at least a bit of French.

Eventually, the entire family began to grasp the unthinkable, and on TJ's 5th birthday, quite understandably, Jaycee could no longer control her grief. She was hospitalized for 13 days, every one of which her father spent with her, as he admitted that he was not completely sure he could ever fully recover from the loss of his grandson, but was quite certain that he could not deal with losing the both of them. He read to her everyday, as she was 'frozen inside herself' the doctors said, and consoled her every night before going home that, whatever the future held, they would face it together, and they would never give up hope.

Jaycee moved home when she was released from the hospital. She refused to continue to take medication that made her feel "numb", so the support of her family, counseling twice a week and what was referred to her as a "profound loss support group" were to be the first blocks in building a new foundation. She was aware that it would be easy to just stay in bed on the bad days if she remained in her own apartment, and the expectation was that there would be more bad days than good for the foreseeable future.

It is exactly at this point, she would admit later, that a support group can make a critical difference in one's outlook. Although there was no anticipation on Jaycee's part that sharing such an experience with strangers would be helpful, and even a bit of fear that it might not be possible, she agreed to attend the weekly sessions.

The group was moderated by the psychologist she was seeing, and comprised of six couples that had experienced the loss of a child.

As comforting as family and friends can be at such a time in one's life, it is often quite surprising, her doctor had advised her, that strangers who can relate to the very same situation can almost immediately provide some tiny form of relief, if only in the realization that others have passed through that very dark place, and the fact that they have survived would have to cause one to think that there just might be worthwhile insight to be had in the exchange.

After Jaycee's introduction to the group, her emotional description of the events leading to her being there had the entire group sobbing. There was not the liberating feeling of unburdening herself of this private nightmare to this attentive group of people, but there was the unexpected comment from one of the mothers that she would always look back to as the touchstone of her healing process. Healing, after all, cannot begin until one believes it is even possible, and in the abyss created by such a tragic event, the central question is really just that; 'Am I capable of surviving this?'.

Most of the discussions among the members of this support group were obviously quite emotional, and the dozen listeners in her audience that evening truly felt her pain. When Jaycee had finished, and a few of the mothers hugged her and attempted to offer heartfelt condolences, one of the mothers asked to say a few words in response.

She spoke of how she interpreted the value of this group coming together under such trying conditions, and that she did not believe there could be anything more painful to deal with than the loss of a child. She pointed out that she was able to take some small comfort in Jaycee's story, and with all due care not to compare such horrible stories or to lessen one person's grief versus another, this stranger spoke about how she was at least relieved that this child survived.

It was the fact that this woman relayed her relief as a 'personal' gain, and came across as not in any way intended to be a comment for Jaycee to consider herself more fortunate than those in the group whose children had died, that caused Jaycee to consider at that moment something beyond the pain of not being with someone she loved so deeply, and to consider the well being of her son.

As all things are relative, Jaycee was aware, and supremely grateful, that she did not live the horror of wondering what evil her son might be enduring. Whatever else, even with the painful prospect of never seeing him again, there was some tiny consolation in the knowledge that he would be looked after with love. Above all else, her former husband loved his son. And, unlike the six other couples who were forced to bid a final goodbye to their children, given up to accidents, cancer and a genetic heart problem, Jaycee could still hold out some shred of hope that, perhaps one day, Bill would come to his senses and allow her son to contact her.

In the two years following that first meeting, Jaycee became good friends with these six couples. They had gotten together socially on many occasions, and now they had gathered at her parent's house, on this cold New England evening, to say goodbyes and to wish her well.

As she and her father went back into the house, and the first of the guests began to leave, Jaycee made an unplanned announcement following a traditional tapping on a glass with a spoon to get everyone's attention. She let them know how grateful she was, and how fortunate she felt to have had their support through these past years.

She assured them that she was not leaving them forever, and in humor said that she may even be back after the first semester at her new job if the new surroundings were not as helpful as she hoped they would be. With that, there were tearful hugs, pleas to stay in touch and offers to fly out to New Mexico "at a moments notice" if she needed help of any kind.

Saying goodbye to her parents, sister, niece and nephew the next morning in her parents driveway proved to be the hardest part, and the point of serious reconsideration, but she eventually got herself into the car and headed out for the long drive across the country.

In order to see things as they truly are,
One must be able to open the eyes and the mind
at the same time.

Chapter Four

Social Studies

It was another beautiful day when Kate saddled Sanchez and started out for the meadow. She took her book along with the good intention of reviewing what she had read the day before. It felt kind of good to actually be ahead for the next session, but since she didn't remember much of it she thought it might not be a bad idea to at least give it a once-over.

She thought a little about Ms. Turner on the ride. The more she got to know her, the more she admired her. She spoke in such an intelligent way, and yet, somehow, she never seemed to be 'showy' about it. This was a real knack, Kate thought, for a teacher. It was her experience that teachers sometimes intimidated students by spouting out facts very familiar to themselves, in a way that often seemed intended to impress more than educate. Kate was religious about taking notes in class, so the challenge for her was always sorting through the 'spouted' facts to find what was needed in order to grasp the real concept of the subject or, at the very least, to sift out the facts that were likely to be part of a test. Ms. Turner, Kate was thinking, made facts seem like they were part of the conversation, like answers to questions Kate had been meaning to ask. For the first time in her short life, Kate found herself giving some consideration to the merits of a career in teaching. Not because it was something she felt she wanted to do, but more to help reverse the long established routine of teachers bringing questions to classes for students to answer. She was suddenly seeing the error in the concept, and the value in the idea of teachers providing answers to questions posed by curious students.

When she arrived at the meadow she could see the lunch sack sticking out from behind the log. Upon opening it to see what she had left inside, she was surprised to see that it was empty, even though she distinctly remembered leaving the other half of the cheese sandwich she didn't finish and a package of peanut butter crackers behind.

It wasn't the fact that the food was gone. She was well aware that there were plenty of animals in these parts that would go to great lengths to enjoy a cheese sandwich. But the bag was still zipped shut when she picked it up. She was puzzled about how an animal could have gotten the thing zipped. Kate had always heard of how clever raccoons and prairie dogs could be, though, and she fully appreciated the reality of one of these critters taking the time to get the bag open. "But, why stay around to close the bag?" she thought to herself.

Just as an experiment, she decided to leave behind some hard candy and an apple she had brought along with her as bait. She tied it all up tightly in a small rawhide pouch that contained the Runes she occasionally tossed when seeking Divine assistance with a tough decision, but dumped those in the saddlebag. After placing the pouch on the log where the lunch bag had been, she chuckled and explained the reason for the bait to Sanchez, who was noticeably unimpressed by the whole idea.

"C'mon boy, whatever got into the lunch bag is going to go crazy trying to untie that pouch. You know if *you* thought of it you would think it was funny too. Anyway, it's time to head on back."

At dinner that evening Kate told her father all about the stargazing session the previous evening. She thought that bringing up the subject would prompt him to talk about how he used to love to look through his telescope, but it didn't. It was clear to her that more prompting was in order.

"Remember when you used to sit me on your lap and have me look through that old telescope out on the front porch, Dad?"

"Yes, I sure do. I spent many an hour out there when you were small. Were you able to impress your tutor with some of the stuff you learned all those years ago?"

"Actually, I think she was a bit surprised that I knew *some* of the stars, but she is *so* intelligent, Dad, I'm sure it would take a lot more than me to impress her," Kate answered.

"I have to say, Kate, first impressions being what they are, in the brief time we spent together at that lunch the other day, I'm inclined to agree. She does seem to be a very intelligent lady. But don't sell yourself short, sweetheart, I consider myself a fairly wise old man, and you impress *me* on a regular basis," her dad said as he stood behind her holding her hair as if making a ponytail.

Kate laughed and said, "Thanks, Dad! And you know I have *always* considered you a wise guy."

"Wise man, sweetheart. Wise *man*," he responded while pretending to pull on the ponytail he was holding.

As her dad sat back down to eat, Kate decided that, since he wasn't offering any reason for giving up the telescope, she was going to have to ask.

"What ever happened to that old telescope, Dad?"

"Oh, I took it to a flea market some years back. I sometimes regret that because I occasionally get a real urge, especially on a perfectly clear evening, to get out there and see what's going on in the universe. But, you know, Kate, your mother and I actually started dating because of our mutual interest in star-gazing, and we spent a lot of time together looking at the night sky. You probably don't remember her being out there as much as me when you were small because she was usually busy getting you ready for bed or cleaning up after me, but I'm convinced she loved stargazing even more than I back then.

"Anyway, after mom was gone, I decided it wasn't the same kind of fun by myself. And I had a lot of difficulty not thinking about her every time I got that old telescope out, so I just gave it up. I must say, though, hearing how excited you were about seeing what you saw last night, I sure wish I had kept it for you."

Kate was holding back tears. This was a typical occurrence whenever her dad's voice went soft while talking about her mother. When this sort of thing happened she usually ended up feeling bad about initiating the conversation, because, although it was definitely getting better every year, she knew it was still difficult for him to have a conversation about life in the days when mom was alive.

Her father reached across the table, took her hand and looked in her eyes.

"Sweetheart," he said, "you don't need to try to spare me from feeling bad about your mother not being here. A lot of time has passed, and I'm quite able to deal with that these days. God knows, I'll always miss her, but you should understand that I came to feel blessed having you there to help fill the void she left. And you are so much like her I swear sometimes it's like she's been reincarnated. If I get a bit pensive every once in awhile when reminiscing about life in those days, it's okay. I always end up appreciating that I had what time I did have with her, and being so thankful that you were a product of that time."

Well, so much for holding in the tears. Kate got out of her chair and hugged her dad around the neck while she wept on his shoulder.

"I wish she was here for you Dad," was all she could manage to say while he held her and gently stroked her long hair.

"I'd probably just be in trouble all the time for spoiling you the way I do," he said in a comforting attempt to lighten the mood.

"Oh my God!" she quickly countered. "If anyone around here has been spoiled it's you, thanks to my doting on you all these years," Kate joked as she wiped her eyes and turned toward the sink to begin the dishes. Since they swapped clean-up duty the evening before, it was her turn, but her dad stayed around to help with the drying.

"So, what's up for tonight, Kate? Big plans?" he inquired after a minute or so of silence.

"As a matter of fact, Mallory is picking me up at 7:30."

"And where, pray tell, is the dynamic duo off to on this lovely Friday evening?"

"I'm not exactly sure, Dad. She was wanting to go to 'The Rack' to see the band, but there's a dance at the rec center tonight, so we will probably end up doing either, or both."

"Is this the band with the kid that likes you?"

"That is *not* why we're going, Dad!" she insisted, "and there is definitely nothing wrong with that memory of yours, is there?"

"There is on occasion, but not when it comes to keeping an eye on my 'one and only' dear," he winked. "Anyway, I'm heading over to Mallory's myself for a little while tonight. I'm going to play some cards with her folks, although I have a feeling they invited me just to introduce me to this woman friend of theirs. You know how they are always trying to fix me up with somebody."

"They're just looking out for ya, Pops," Kate laughed. "Now you go and have a good time, but don't be out too late!"

"Very funny, dear. You have fun, be careful, and I'll see you later!"

"The Rack" was a really big place. It was a meeting hall turned into a bar. The dance floor was huge, and Friday nights the place was always packed with teens because it was no alcohol night. The story goes that when the owner petitioned the town for a license to open the oversized bar, the commission stipulated that a liquor license would be granted if the owner agreed to voluntarily maintain one night each week as a non-alcohol night for young people. The idea was a good one for both sides. The kids from town, and several surrounding towns, had someplace to hang out on Friday nights, with no drinking involved. The $4.00 cover more than paid for the band, and the cokes, pizza and hot dogs usually generated enough of a profit for the owner to make it a worthwhile evening.

When Mallory and Kate walked in, The Hombres were wrapping up a set with the old, but ever popular, Door's version of "Light My Fire", and, although the vocals were closer to Jim Nabors than Jim Morrison, Cola had the crowd moving to the wailing keyboard, which was more than loud enough to compensate.

During the break Randy brought Keith and Cola over to the table that Mallory and Kate were sharing with some friends. Mallory had called Diane and asked her to save a couple of seats for them. Randy said hello to

Kate as he put his arms around Mallory from behind and kissed her neck.

"Hey Randy," Kate smiled, "nice sound up there!"

"You remember Keith & Cola, right?" he asked as he gestured toward the two boys next to him.

Kate said a quick "Hi" to each and introduced the three of them to Jen and Diane across the table. At no time during the break did Keith speak. Of course, competing with Cola and Randy for time was no small task.

When the band took the stage again, Diane let Mallory know that she was definitely interested in Keith and asked if she knew whether he was seeing anyone. Although Mal didn't let on about Keith having a thing for Kate, she definitely had an obvious kind of 'I know something you don't know' look on her face, and simply told her that she *thought* he was seeing someone, but wasn't sure exactly who it was.

Having worked her way through the crowd to the bar, Kate was waiting patiently for a couple of cokes, and staring into the mirror, which ran the entire length of the wall behind the bar. Just as she cocked her head to make sure her hair looked okay she realized that she recognized the face next to hers in the mirror. When she realized he was staring at her, she winced with embarrassment.

"It looks fine to me, Kate," Daniel said, almost yelling to be heard over the music.

"What?" Kate asked.

"Your hair. It looks fine to me," he explained.

"Oh! Sorry, can't be near a mirror without checking you know." Kate said, blushing. "God," Kate thought, "at least I wasn't checking my teeth."

"So, who are you with?" Daniel inquired.

"Mallory, Jen and um….oh yeah, Diane," she answered as she looked back at the table to remember who else was sitting there.

After he smiled and gave a nod of acknowledgment, the few awkward seconds of silence were, thankfully, broken by the timely appearance of one of the bartenders.

"What'll it be sweetheart?" bellowed the very large person behind the wide wooden bar.

The 'Rack', appropriately named for the pool games that took place upstairs, boasted the longest bar in the State of New Mexico. A hundred people could probably stand at the bar and not be at all cramped. Kate had been told by Mallory, who had been told by Randy, that the guy who owned the place grew up in Dallas and had been inspired by big Texas bars like "Gilley's", and "Billy Bob's".

Kate ordered the two cokes and had them within a few seconds, or so it seemed.

"Let me get those!" Daniel insisted as he tossed a couple of dollars toward the bartender before Kate could even dig the money out of her jeans pocket.

"Well, thanks. But, you didn't have to do that."

After more awkward silence Kate picked up the drinks and said she probably ought to be getting back to her table.

"Yeah, I'd better go find Eden. She was around here somewhere," Daniel said as he turned to give Kate room to move away from the bar.

"Good talking to you, Daniel."

"Really nice running into you too, Kate. See ya in school before long, hey?"

Kate smiled and rolled her eyes in a 'don't remind me' gesture. She said a goodbye that she sort of knew was too soft to be heard over the music as she squeezed by him, trying to keep the cokes from spilling. Just then, the person with his back to her shifted as she moved by, and caused her to lean hard against Daniel to keep her balance. For an instant her shoulder and arm were up against his chest, and her face was only an inch or so from his neck. The senses of touch and smell were magnified enough to have taken up any energy that her hearing might have warranted. At that moment there was no sound in the room. There was only the feel of him next to her, and the sensation that she was floating.

He put his hands on her shoulders to keep her from falling and, even in the unexpected daze created by the close proximity, she was able to regain perfect balance, make a humorous comment about the talent it took to not spill the drinks that took so long to get, and still muster a confident smile as she turned to walk away. Given the spinning that was taking place in her head the graceful exit was almost certainly just good luck.

Kate was approached by a chunky guy with bad skin, who seemed to appear out of nowhere, as she was weaving her way back through the crowd with a coke in each hand. He had intentionally blocked her path in an apparent attempt to pose as some sort of human tollbooth, and told her that he wouldn't let her by until she danced with him. She explained that she preferred dancing without a handful of beverages, and had to deliver the drinks to her friends, but he persisted. Balking at the offer he made to deliver the drinks if she waited for him on the dance floor, Kate was able to finally negotiate the toll down to giving him her phone number.

"You don't have to write it down, my number's in the book," she said, rather smugly, as she maneuvered to the side to get around him.

"But, I don't know your name," he called after her.

"It's in there too!", she shouted without looking back.

Kate finally made her way back to the table, and never answered Mal when she asked about what had taken so long. But, for the rest of the evening she was noticeably preoccupied. Part of the time was spent thinking about how good a couple Daniel and Eden made. Eden was one of those girls that made glasses look cool. Along with being one of the best looking girls in school, she had the second best grade average, behind Daniel of course.

The next morning, as Kate reviewed the highlights of the night, it came to her that she may have seemed very rude to Keith when he returned to her table after playing the last set. She remembered that he was actually speaking to her, which must have taken a lot of courage as shy as he was, but she had no idea what they talked about.

She remembered that on the way home Mallory told her that she had overheard him ask her to 'go out' sometime. She also remembered Mallory saying that it was like he was talking to someone in a trance. Kate was not one to hurt people's feelings, so the guilt she was feeling about Keith served to temper the enjoyment she should have felt about the Daniel interlude, however brief.

Anyway, there was no time to do anything about it now. It was going to be a pretty full Saturday. After finishing in the barn, she planned to exercise Sanchez with a quick ride up to the meadow to see if anything got into the pouch of food she left, and be back in time to meet dad at 10:00. She promised to go down to Albuquerque with him to see the horse that he was offered.

Kate felt goose bumps on the back of her neck as she picked the pouch up off the log. When she saw that the string had been untied, and the wrappers from the hard candy put back in the pouch, it was now clear that it wasn't an animal that she had baited. Someone had found her secret place.

As much as she felt surprised that someone could have been there, in *her* place, she had always pretty much known that she couldn't possibly have been the only one to come here to enjoy this meadow. Thinking for a fleeting moment, though, that someone may have watched her while she was there, or even *be* watching her, made her feel suddenly uneasy, so she jumped back on Sanchez and raced off without looking back.

By the time her dad got home and hooked up the horse trailer to leave, she decided against letting him know about the incident for now. She had convinced herself that it was probably just another rider, or a hiker that had come upon that spot and thought that it was a free snack left for anyone that found it. She really wanted to know if the person was just passing through or was a regular visitor of the place that she came to think belonged to her, so she spent some of the time during the drive devising a plan to find out.

The quarter horse that her dad brought her to see was a truly beautiful animal, jet black all over except for a white diamond marking on her face, and a grayish mane. Kate rode her around a bit, and confirmed that she was very well trained and pleasant mannered.

Her dad told the people he would be happy to keep it for them while they tried to sell it, but they insisted that he take the horse for free and give it a good home. The woman that owned the horse told Kate that the one regret she had about moving east was giving up "Duchess." But, she knew it would be some consolation if she could leave with confidence that the horse would be properly cared for. Kate could relate to how badly the woman must have felt giving up this animal, so she did her best to comfort her a little by telling her about Sanchez, and assured her that Duchess would love his company.

The lady seemed genuinely happier when Kate's dad wrote his address down for her, and told her to write anytime if she wanted to hear how the horse was getting along.

On the way home her dad asked if Kate still thought it was a good idea to approach Jaycee Turner about the boarding arrangement. She assured him that *anyone* would have to be thrilled with this beautiful animal.

"It's not only a great looking horse, Dad, but it seems to have a perfect temperament for a novice rider," she told him. "I'm sure Ms. Turner would be absolutely shocked to get *any* horse of her own, much less one like this."

It struck Kate as she said it that, although it was put in the context of a business question, she couldn't help thinking that her dad was really asking whether Ms. Turner would *like* the horse. "There may be more interest in her teacher than he lets on," she thought to herself.

On Sunday Kate had hoped to get back up to the meadow to ease her curiosity. But, the day came and went with too many things going to afford the time.

At 9:30 on Monday morning, after finishing all that she needed to get done, she put a few more snacks in a lunch bag and got ready to go. Just as she was headed out the door the phone rang.

It was Ms. Turner asking if it would be okay to change the class that was scheduled for Tuesday to *this* morning around 11:00, because something came up and she wouldn't be back in time on the following day.

So much for plans. "Sure," she obliged. "I can do it."

"Oh, that's great, Kate. I really do appreciate your flexibility with this. Hopefully I won't ever have to reschedule again with this short a notice. I'll be by to get you around eleven then." Ms. Turner acknowledged.

The lunch bag was put back in the refrigerator for later, just in case there might still be time to get up to the meadow when she got back.

At one point, near the end of the session, Kate was pacing behind the sofa at Ms. Turner's house answering questions about the reading assignment. During a pause she found herself staring at a photograph of a young boy that was on the bookcase. She had noticed it before but hadn't paid much attention to it. As she stared at the picture, though, she could see that there were very striking similarities between the child and Ms. Turner.

"Is this a nephew?" Kate asked as she pointed at the picture.

After looking to see what Kate was referring to, Ms. Turner's expression changed, and following an uncomfortable silence, she looked from the photograph to Kate and spoke in a most serious tone.

"No," she said very somberly. "As a matter of fact, that is my son. After an uncomfortable pause, Jaycee looked at Kate and said, "Actually, he is a part of my life that I don't speak much about these days. I guess I have tried hard to keep people from knowing about that side of my personal life, so that I wouldn't have to come up with a way to answer questions about it."

"God, I'm so sorry Ms. Turner," an embarrassed Kate apologized. "I never meant to pry."

"No, no, honestly Kate, that's fine. It is a perfectly innocent question, and it deserves an honest answer," admitted Jaycee. "I'm going to trust you with a story that I would prefer not to be the talk of the school cafeteria. I know you are mature for your age, so I won't concern myself with that possibility."

The fact that Jaycee Turner, one of the adults she most respected, considered her "mature" enough to entrust her with a personal secret gave Kate an immediate feeling of overwhelming pride and privilege. She had never felt more responsible than she did at that moment. Kate positioned herself so that she was facing her teacher, attentively, in the easy chair directly across from her.

Ms. Turner began the story by telling her that she had lived in Massachusetts prior to moving to New Mexico.

"I got married shortly after college graduation, to a boy that I had known for only ten months. He was finishing law school when I met him, and in a little more than a year after we were married we had a son, Timothy Jackson Turner. But, from the time I first held him, I always called him TJ.

"By the time our son was three, my husband and I were having real compatibility problems. The only saving grace was that he began a job with the Government, based in Massachusetts and traveling back and forth to Washington a lot, so he wasn't around all that much. We made the common mistake early in the marriage of thinking a shaky relationship could be improved with the sharing of a child. Unfortunately, while we did both find true joy with our son, it didn't improve our feelings for one another. We had either *become* very different people, or just didn't notice how different we were in the 10 months of dating.

"My mother took care of the baby while I was doing graduate work during the day, and I spent the evenings studying with T.J. on my lap. I remember missing him like crazy, even if I was only away for a few hours."

Kate's excitement about being spoken to as an adult was fading quickly as Jaycee Turner's voice became more somber. It was replaced with a sense of dread that, since the boy in the photograph was being spoken about in the past tense, she was about to be told of something very tragic. At that moment, she wondered if she might soon regret having heard the story at all.

"To make a long and complicated story as short as possible, things got progressively worse with Bill and I as he got more involved with his job.

"He started drinking a lot, working twelve-hour days, and sometimes not even coming home on weekends, and it seemed we argued about almost everything. When I finally couldn't bear to live with him anymore, I asked him to consider a temporary separation while he got his life back in order, but he made it clear that he was not beyond taking 'violent action' if I ever tried to take his son away from him.

"Eventually I moved out and got an apartment for my son and I, and began the process of a temporary legal separation. It was a pretty ugly time for everyone in my family because Bill was so hostile. Since he was very familiar with the law, he was assuring my parents and I that he would easily win custody of T.J., and that he would do it by proving I was an unfit mother if necessary.

"I still don't know if I was fortunate, or unfortunate when we finally made it to court. I did retain full custody of our son, but Bill was able to get very liberal visitation rights, even though there was a restraining order invoked so he couldn't be around me. So, it was arranged that he was picking up T.J. at my sister's for his visits. I really should have understood that this process would be extremely aggravating to him at the time. I've come to know that it is just this oversight that has been so frustrating to me over the years. Saying that Bill was one that didn't take losing very well would be a gross understatement.

On T.J.'s fourth birthday, Bill said he was taking the whole day off to be with him so he planned to pick him up early and get him back to my sister's in time for dinner. Well, he never came back, and I haven't seen either of them since.

"The last time I saw my son was when I got him up on that morning of his birthday, before I dropped him off at my sister's house. I later found out that Bill had been planning to take him away for some time. His work in the state government gave him access to all the information he needed about changing identities, so he was pretty well prepared to do what he did.

"Anyway, for the next couple of years I went through every cent I earned, and some of my parent's money, hiring private detectives to find my son. It didn't seem feasible to me, at first, that a man and a four-year old boy could just 'hide'. I kept thinking at the time that there would eventually have to be a doctor for the boy or, at the very least, there would be a school enrollment in the next year. But, understanding that as time passed the odds of finding him decreased, I grew more and more despondent as I became less and less hopeful.

"I was finally advised that any further searching would probably be futile, and that it was conceivable, with changed names, my husband and my son were likely living in another country.

"For almost four years, I lived with an obsession. Except for attending classes, every waking moment was spent exploring leads, talking to investigators, making calls to school administrators systems, or just looking at maps to try to figure out where to look next. Toward the end of that time, when I finally began to realize that he had really gotten away with it, I knew that I needed to try begin to heal, and the only way I thought I could do that was to move away, or, I felt I would just continue to be consumed by a combination of grief and bitterness.

I always wanted to live in the west, so I got out a map, did a bit of job prospecting by phone, and decided to move, and, well, here I am.

When she stopped speaking, and looked up at Kate, she saw that her eyes were full of tears. She walked over and sat next to her.

"Kate, I didn't mean to make you sad with all this. I'm sure I shouldn't have burdened you with this whole story. I just didn't want to lie to you about it."

Doing all she could to maintain her composure, Kate responded "I can't believe it. That's just awful, Ms. Turner!"

"Yes, I know, dear. It *is* awful. But, don't you be sad for me, Kate. I have already had my years of dealing with the worst of it, and although I still think about him many times every day, I believe I have come to grips with the possibility of not ever seeing him again. Though I will never give up hope of that, I am able to at least take some comfort in knowing that he is being looked after, probably doing okay. His father obviously loved him very much to go to such extreme measures to be with him. So, I'm quite confident he would take very good care of him.

Now, come on let's get your stuff, your father will be here any minute!"

Neither spoke for the several minutes it took for Kate to pick up her papers and put them back in her notebook. Kate couldn't say goodbye when she left. She knew she would cry again if she spoke. Instead, when her father arrived she quickly picked up her things, turned and gave Ms. Turner a long hug without speaking, spun back toward the door and ran out to meet her ride. It was an awkward exit, and the more she thought about it during the ride home the more embarrassed she felt.

It was pretty quiet in the car that night. It might have been a good night for one of the show tune tapes, which she would have been able to ignore completely. But, for some reason the only 'rock' tape her dad owned was playing when she got in the car; and before he had driven a few hundred yards, the distinct lead in to "I Know You're Out There Somewhere" echoed from the speakers. It was a song she had heard many times, and never thought of it as a sad song. But, on this night those words, of *all* words, and of *all* nights, served to bring the stifled emotions right back into her throat. At first she tried to look out the window so her dad wouldn't notice, but in less than a minute she was trying to disguise her sobbing with a hand over her mouth, until she finally cried out loud.

"Katelynn? Sweetheart?" her dad called out in concern while he pulled the car over to the shoulder.

"What happened tonight, Kate?" he asked as he moved across the seat to comfort her.

"Just a really sad story, Dad," Kate choked out, tears streaming down her face, "and it really shouldn't even bother me this much. But the music just...., I don't know, but I don't think I can talk about it right now."

"That's fine with me, sweetheart. You know I'll listen when you want to tell me. As long as you're okay," he said, and he held her head on his shoulder while he assured her that it was perfectly okay to cry.

In a few minutes when Kate regained her composure, she told him she felt pretty stupid.

"There's absolutely nothing to feel stupid about, sweetheart. Sometimes things just pile up, and the next thing you know, the emotions you thought you had under control are right there at the surface again."

"Well, anyway, thanks for understanding that I just don't want to talk about it now, Dad," she said as she straightened up her face with some tissues from the glove compartment.

"Anytime!" he acknowledged as he slid back over to the wheel and eased the car back onto the road. "And by the way, Katelynn dear, about the music. There's nothing sad about the 'Moody Blues'."

That brought a smile, and an end, to the conversation, until each said goodnight shortly after getting home that night.

What is it that we recognize
in those we do not know?
Could it be the secret lies,
in lives lived long ago?

Chapter Five

Philosophy

At breakfast, Kate related to her father the whole story she had heard the night before. She told him that Ms. Turner hoped that it wouldn't be circulated through the town, so she was sure to emphasize that she trusted him to tell no one.

"Wow, Kate. No wonder you were sad last night. That's just an incredible story. I have trouble even believing it could have happened. Good Lord, she must suffer every day.

"I still don't know, though, if I agree with her burdening someone your age with that kind of story."

"Like I said, Dad, I'm not exactly sure I would have asked once I knew, and I am absolutely sure she had no intention to have that discussion, but I feel good that she trusted me to be mature enough to handle it, and to keep it private."

Her father agreed that her teacher must have considered her very mature, and trustworthy, to have shared such a personal thing with her.

After breakfast, Kate rushed through the barn chores to get Sanchez saddled for the ride to the meadow. Today was the day to find out who, or what, was intruding on her sacred territory.

She put the lunch bag and a pair of binoculars in the saddlebag, and she was off.

"Going for a ride this early?" asked her dad as he eyed her walking Sanchez out of the barn.

"Yep, I'm off to the meadow for a bit. But, I won't be gone long. See you for lunch."

"Okay. Be careful!" he shouted as she trotted away.

The phone was ringing as he watched her turn out of sight. It was Jaycee Turner.

"Hello, Michael?"

"Yes it is," he answered. "Hi! This is Jaycee, how are you?"

"Fine thanks. And you, Jaycee?"

"Good too, thanks. Is Kate at home?" she asked.

"No, you just missed her. She's out for a ride. Can I give her a message for you?"

"Um, I guess not. I just wanted to talk to her," Jaycee stated, her voice echoing her concern.

"I do expect her back for lunch. Would you like me to have her call you then?" he asked.

After she hesitated long enough that he was convinced she was more than likely worried about Kate, he continued; "Look, Jaycee, why don't you come out here and see her when she gets back. I'll even throw in one of my special sandwiches to make your travel worthwhile. There's something Kate and I have been wanting to show you anyway."

"I think I would really like that, if you're sure it wouldn't be interfering with your day."

"Not at all. I'll look forward to seeing you about noon. How's that?" he confirmed.

"Thanks Michael. I'll be there."

"This is probably good," he thought to himself, "it's good that she is probably concerned it was more than Kate needed to hear, and now that Kate *does* know it might help her feel a little less horrible about it by talking it out some more."

The wind was creating a lot of noise in the trees as Kate made her way down the path to the meadow. It was a cloudy morning, not the threatening kind of sky that would normally precede a storm, but enough of an overcast that, combined with new consideration of the chance that someone could actually be watching her, it made the tree covered pathway seem much darker than she was used to seeing it. Getting to the point where the path opened to the meadow provided a slight relief, and a quick scan of the area made her feel somewhat comfortable that everything appeared to be undisturbed.

She walked Sanchez to the spot where she had left the food before, set the lunch bag on the log and turned him back toward the path leading home. He seemed quite confused about not getting the usual time to take in some of the tall grass, but followed along just the same. From the trail that they usually took up and down the incline there was another much smaller path that led completely around the meadow and continued up a fairly steep hill to an overlook. When she walked Sanchez up as far as she could safely go, and tied him off behind some brush, she got out the binoculars and nestled in behind a large rock. From there she could clearly see the part of the meadow where she had left the bait even without the binoculars, but the 60 yards or so of distance was brought in much clearer with them.

For about 20 minutes Kate waited behind that rock, occasionally looking up from the book she brought to read, looking and listening for any sign of movement.

"How do I know this person doesn't come at night?" she finally thought to herself in frustration. "Or maybe they watch when I come here and only come for the food after they see me leave. Heck, who knows if they would even come back?" And just in the moment she was pretty much convinced that it was probably ridiculous to spend any more time on the possible coincidence that the food snatcher would show up while she had the place staked out, she was certain she heard something. In the next few seconds, as she remained still and held her breath to listen, she was certain there was a rustling, and it was close by.

She suddenly had the sensation that the air around her was pressing on her skin as she tried to listen with all of her senses, and in the following moments the sound of her own thundering pulse in her ears made the listening seem as though she was underwater. Her first thought, still not breathing, was how foolish it was to be there, alone.

When she was able to move, she raised the binoculars to her eyes and quickly swept the meadow for the source of what she thought she heard.

"Oh Captain, my Captain?" a voice echoed from directly behind her.

Kate turned so quickly she hit the binoculars on the rock with a whack and dropped her book. Her heart felt as though it was imploding when she realized there was a person five feet away from her. Her vision was blurred, but she could see that it was a man hunched over with his hands on his knees, straining to see what she was viewing.

The scare caused her throat to close. It was as though she was frozen between breaths while her brain seemed to take forever to sort out what was going on, and what the reaction should be. As the shock turned to fear, somewhere in the transition she thought she felt herself scream, but if so it was from instinct, and it wasn't successful. Her mouth definitely opened, but nothing came out.

"Oh, jeez, I guess I scared you, didn't I? Please…, I'm so sorry. Really, no need to be afraid!" said the stranger as he backed away with his hands showing in a peaceful manner. "I was just wondering what you were doing up here. Are you okay?"

Thankful that she had gotten the breathing process restarted while he apologized, and having had a chance to look at him, and hear his apology, the fear she had felt began to slowly fade. But, within what was really only a matter of five or ten seconds from the time she first detected this unexpected intruder, her nervous system had gone to full alert from the alarm sounded by her brain, and reversing this process worked a bit more slowly.

Easing back against the rock on which she had been leaning prior to the scare, and holding her chest in an attempt to slow her heartbeat, she could feel that her face was fully flushed. That small part of her that wasn't half frightened to death was becoming embarrassed about being caught unawares.

"Oh God! You scared the b'jeezus out of me!" she blurted out. "What are you doing here? Who are you? What did you say?"

"I really didn't mean to startle you like that, honestly. I saw you there, watching so intently, and I was just wondering what was down there," the stranger said sheepishly. "You can call me Elijah, and I was just quoting my favorite Whitman poem. That is Walt Whitman you were reading, yes?"

As he spoke, and as her senses began to return to normal with the slightly slowing heartbeat, Kate noticed that he had a different kind of voice. It was a very soothing kind of tone, which was just what the situation called for.

He was dressed in a navy blue T-shirt, jeans and work boots. There was almost something familiar about him, she thought, though she was sure she had never met him. Facing the sun, his boyish face was lit up by the most striking, crystal-like, gray eyes, which were fixed on her with a most apologetic look. The light beard covering his chin and the way his hair stuck up in a sort of planned disarray made it difficult to guess his age. He seemed as though he could be near her age, she thought at first, but may well be several years older. As she stared at him, she noticed Sanchez peeking at her from behind him.

"What is with *you?*" she yelled at the horse. "You *never* let anyone else near you. And now you let a perfect stranger sneak up behind me and you don't even make a sound?"

"Well, perhaps not perfect, but a good stranger for sure," he said with a comforting grin. "Anyway, I tend to get along well with animals. They have a good sense about whether people intend them any harm. So, tell me, what's so important down there?"

"It's just food," she said while giving the sulking Sanchez a cold stare.

"Yeah, I guess I kind of knew that. I meant, what is it that you brought? Anything good?"

All of a sudden her attention snapped back to this boy.

"It's *you?*" she gasped. "*You're* the one taking the food?"

"Well, accepting the food I think is more accurate. After all, there was no note or card left that made it seem for anyone in particular. Was it intended for someone else?" he asked innocently.

"No! No, it wasn't meant for anyone. I mean, at first it was just left by mistake..., then it was sort of an experiment, I thought it must be an animal..., after that I...," Kate answered realizing she was making very little sense.

"I see," he interjected. "So am I who you're looking for then? I mean, with the binoculars? Am I your experiment?"

"I didn't know what to expect. I guess I....What are you doing out here anyway?" she demanded.

Elijah told her that he was making his way across the State, and that he stopped in this area partly because he had always heard how scenic it was. Once he found the food that first day, he decided he would stay a few more days to see if there might be more treats. He said he really enjoyed the things she left.

"So, you happened by *this* place and found *my* lunch and decided to make yourself at home?" she asked, getting to her feet.

"Uh, yes. That's about right," he admitted, his eyebrows raised in an apologetic furl.

"Elijah what?" Kate asked.

"Actually no."

"Elijah No?" she clarified.

"No, I meant 'actually no' it's not Elijah *What*. It's just Elijah."

"Are you famous Just Elijah, like Cher, where everyone knows who you are by your first name?" she mused.

"Well," he replied after thinking for a moment, "would I be the only Elijah *you* know?"

After Kate admitted that he would, in fact, be the only one she knew, he told her that there wouldn't seem, then, to be a need for adding another name. She, of course, quickly countered that she would surely meet another person named Elijah *one day*, and have no way to refer to each without confusion. To which Elijah responded that, hopefully, the next one would have a last name, and that would suffice to solve the problem.

"Let's start over, without the scare, shall we?" he said, approaching her with his hand out in a sign of peace. "I don't get to speak to many people lately, so I would just as soon not spend it bickering."

"Hello, lunch maker." Elijah smiled. "I'm *very* pleased to make your acquaintance, and very grateful for the things you left for me. I've really enjoyed them."

Kate took his hand, shook it lightly, smiled, and said, "I'm Kate, and you're welcome, I guess. I'm sorry if it seemed I was arguing. I suppose I get a bit testy when someone scares me half to death and then refuses to even give a name," she finished with a tone that reflected a hint of sarcasm.

They walked down the hill, Sanchez in tow, to the log where she had left the lunch, and both sat down as he opened the bag to see what was inside.

"Oh, Jeez Louise, Twinkies! I don't even believe it. Do you know how long it's been since I have had a Twinkie?" he beamed.

"I'm sure I don't," she answered. "But if I can't know your last name, perhaps I should take it back."

"Whitman?" he quickly offered.

"Elijah *Whitman*?" Kate said with more that a little doubt.

"That would seem a coincidence, wouldn't it, given the "Oh Captain?" she asked.

"And – did you say *Jeez Louise*? You really *aren't* from around here, are you? How about we just sit down a bit, while you enjoy that snack, and tell me what you are doing passing through here. Where are you staying? Where did you come from, and any other details you feel open to sharing Mr. *Whitman*?"

"As a matter of fact, I've been staying in what appears to be a currently unoccupied hunting cabin not very far from here, which is actually quite cozy." he explained. "And, I admit my name isn't Whitman, but I love his work.

"I came from out east, so I've been traveling a good while."

Elijah went on to tell Kate about having been on the road, alone, making his way across the country. He told her how great it had been to have some time to really think about things, and to be able to see places he had only heard or read about. He said that he had some time to get where he needed to be, so he was "taking the time to enjoy the journey."

Kate found herself to be very intrigued by this stranger. She had never met anyone so free spirited, or so apparently carefree, and she wondered how old he was because, although he looked as though he could be close to her age, he spoke as though he were much older.

"Did you leave college to travel around then?" she asked.

"Mmm, what a taste," he moaned as he finished the second Twinkie. "Odd isn't it, how the simple things like cream filled cakes can make for such a pleasurable experience?"

"I don't really give them much thought, Kate admitted. "I don't even like them. Those were my dad's."

"Don't *like* them?" he questioned while shaking his head. "And you seem like someone who appreciates the finer things. Anyway, I wasn't actually speaking strictly about the Twinkies there, Kate. I meant *all* things like that. All these little things that provide such simple pleasures. They sure get easy to appreciate once we go without them. In any case, I'm glad that your dad is a man of good taste. And, to belatedly address the question, no. I didn't get to college."

"Where did you go to high school, back east?" she pressed.

"Well, I went to a couple, actually. Last one was Classical High, in Massachusetts. Ever hear of it?" he answered with a question.

"No. Should I have?"

"I don't suppose so. Anyway, what about you? When you're not riding your horse around the countryside leaving food for poor drifters, are you in school, Miss Kate?" he inquired.

"Well, school doesn't open until next week, but yes, I'm a senior," she offered.

"That would be *high school* senior, right?" he quizzed.

"Do I look like I might be a college senior?" she asked in a sarcastic tone.

"Now, that's one of those questions with no acceptable answer, isn't it?" he said while rubbing his chin in a pondering gesture. "I think that my intelligence is limited when it comes to knowing at what age a woman stops wanting to hear that she looks older than she is. In the circle of knowledge, that would be one of those 'I know that I don't know' categories, and a dangerous one at that, so I think I'll pass."

"Circle of knowledge?" Kate inquired.

"You haven't gone through eleven years of formal schooling without covering the circle of knowledge, have you?" he asked with his eyes fixed to hers.

He detected in her hesitation that she might be slightly embarrassed to admit her ignorance of something he had made to sound so basic, so just as she opened her mouth to answer he added, "I guess they have crammed the curriculum with too much other stuff to have enough room for some of the basic philosophy anymore.

"In a nutshell, though," Elijah explained, "there are those that subscribe to a theory that only three categories exist, which include all of everything there is to know.

One very small wedge of this circle would be that which we *already* know, and I personally believe we tend to constantly overestimate this portion. Another somewhat larger segment would be what each of us knows that we *don't* know, say like Swahili, or exactly how a television works, calculus or whether 'Big Foot' really roams the 'forest Primeval'. These are the two categories of knowledge in which the majority of us spend our whole lives.

"The last behemoth chunk, though," he fashioned a pie shaped figure with his hands that would easily be half of a circle, "this is what we don't even know we don't know. This is where inventions originate. Where creativity is born. It is also the place where what *could* be known occasionally gets blocked by what is *believed*."

Kate sat and stared after he stopped speaking. She was somewhere between hypnotized and dumbfounded. There was a kind of sermon induced core dump that was taking place in her brain. She understood exactly what he had been talking about, but it was taking longer than usual to sort it out. She found herself to be somewhat spellbound by the way he spoke so passionately about something that might actually have been boring if presented differently.

"Sorry," he said as he rolled his eyes. "Sometimes I just go off. You have to understand that I don't get to speak to people that much these days."

"Yeah, you mentioned that," Kate added curiously, hoping to prompt him to explain.

"You know, Just Elijah, I would definitely like to know more about this journey of yours. But, I really have to get going now. I promised my dad I would be home for lunch.

"Why don't you come back *with* me, I mean back to my house for a real meal?

"I'm sure my dad would even let you stay a couple of days if you needed a place. He's great like that. You would like him," she assured him as she stood up from the log and whistled for Sanchez.

"That's definitely a very generous gesture there, my new friend, but I'm afraid that would interfere with my *outdoor experience* here. I'll tell you what, though, I have really enjoyed talking to you. I plan to hang around these parts for a little while longer, so if you get a chance to come back by here in the next couple of days, maybe we can meet again. And, if by chance, it happened that you came back to visit and had some kind of potato chips with you at the time, well, I would definitely have to consider myself doubly blessed," he said as he smiled and stood up.

As much as Kate thought it was a rather bold request to ask for her to bring him food if she happened to come back, she quickly satisfied herself that the request was made in jest. "What about tomorrow?" Kate asked as she pulled herself up onto the saddle.

"It happens I'm free tomorrow," he replied as he ran his hand along the horse's neck. "Now, take the lady home, faithful steed, and tarry not in the forest along the way, rain is approaching," he said in a voice intended to sound noble. "And thanks for not giving me away back there," he added in more of a whisper.

"So, there's a Sancho in the bloodline is there?" he asked. "Sanchez generally means son of Sancho in Spanish, no?"

"Yes, actually. His sire was Sancho. That was my Dad's horse, but I'm still amazed at how he has taken to you. He's not usually like this you know. Definitely not with strangers," Kate informed him. "I'll try to come back around the same time. Are you sure you're okay out here? Do you need anything?"

"Really, thanks for your concern, but I'm fine," he assured her.

"See you tomorrow then!" With that Kate nudged Sanchez into a full turn and headed back down the trail.

"Drive safely!" she heard from behind as she rode away.

All the way back she thought about Elijah. How he just seemed to *appear* out of nowhere. She wondered how she could feel so comfortable with him, knowing nothing about him. "He could be running away from the law for all I know," she thought out loud, "why else would he not want me to know his last name?" she wondered.

Somehow, in her heart, she had this absolute faith that he was harmless. But, more importantly, she had a very *different* feeling about him, one that she was wrestling with figuring out. It wasn't just the curiosity. There was no doubt in her mind, having spent less than an hour with him, that she had never met anyone like him before. He seemed very confident and worldly, but what struck her, after giving the matter more thought, was that what really set him most apart from all the boys that she knew was how unguarded he seemed to be. "Maybe it's just that he seems so much more natural," she thought. He wasn't different in a way she could describe, exactly. But she was sure that no boy *she* knew would ever act excited about something like a Twinkie, unless they were kidding around of course. Boys that she knew didn't normally risk the possibility of looking less than 'macho'. At least not intentionally.

Sanchez, of course, had no answer when she asked him again why he made no sound when this stranger was sneaking up on her. He was concentrating on the terrain at the time, and seemed to realize that she would choose to answer the question herself.

"You saw something harmless there, didn't ya boy?" she acknowledged on his behalf. "Well, I trust your instinct. But, just so you understand, I want to be warned about *everyone* sneaking up on me from now on, not just the ones that *you* think might be dangerous. Is that understood? For now, though, we definitely need to know more about this mystery man, and I need to figure out how to do that by tomorrow."

At just about half way back, the wind started picking up and Kate could see rain coming toward her from the west. She remembered Elijah telling Sanchez something about rain, but wasn't paying much attention. Her first thought was that it probably would be impossible for him to make it back to where ever he was staying before getting wet, and it made her feel a bit sad to picture him walking along in the rain.

As they made the turn along the trail where her house came into view, Kate could see that there was an extra car in the driveway. By that time, she had Sanchez in a full trot because the incline wasn't as bad. She firmly pulled back the reigns while reaching into the saddlebag for the binoculars and came to a stop to see who was visiting.

"*Damn it!*" she said out loud as she looked through the binoculars toward the house. What she saw was a fine crack running across the left lens. She did remember hitting them on the rock when she turned to see who was behind her, but in the midst of the excitement of being scared half to death she didn't really think to check them.

The fact that she hadn't asked to take them is what made her feel especially guilty. Her father was always very forgiving about these sorts of things, but he was definitely going to remind her that "the key word that separates borrowing from stealing is permission".

Within a half of a minute of looking through the one good lens, she could see that the car was Ms. Turner's. Hers was an easy car to recognize because it was the only 1966 white Mustang convertible in town, and she kept it looking like it was brand new. She had told Kate that she bought it right after graduating from high school, and could just never come to part with it. Kate thought that it was about as cool a car as she had ever seen up close.

In the space of a couple of seconds after recognizing the car, she had the sinking feeling that she might have forgotten about a tutoring appointment, but quickly assured herself that no such arrangement had been made.

When she turned back toward the west, she was surprised to see that the clouds had gotten so much closer so quickly. She knew it was going to be a challenge to get home before getting wet. Sticking the binoculars back in the saddlebag and pulling her hat down tightly on her forehead, she told Sanchez that the stroll was over and gently prodded him with both heels to get him into a gallop toward home.

"Maybe dad called her to look at the horse," she thought. He *could* have called her, knowing that Kate would be home around lunchtime, to come out for a look. "But, how would he have invited her without giving away the surprise," she wondered.

As she got closer and slowed Sanchez to a trot, she could see her dad and Ms. Turner sitting on the front porch. Just as she acknowledged her dad's wave, she made the decision not to mention anything about Elijah. She was pretty sure that he would not be as confident as she and the horse about how harmless this stranger might be. She never faulted him for it, but she was well aware that being a parent made it mandatory to lean to the side of caution in these matters.

Making a quick dismount at the entrance to the corral, Kate let Sanchez take a long drink from the water trough, tied him up quickly inside the barn and decided to come back to unsaddle him after she went to greet her visitor.

"Well, sweetheart, I was hoping you would show up pretty soon. I thought you were going to get caught in that rain heading this way, and by the looks of the lather on that colt's, neck you had to push him a bit to beat it.

"Jaycee here stopped by and has something she wants to talk to you about," her dad announced in a serious manner.

"Hello, Kate!" Ms. Turner immediately followed.

After Kate had made her greeting, and her apology for being a little late, her dad excused himself from the porch saying he was going to put together some sandwiches for lunch and "leave the girls to talk."

Ms. Turner seemed very timid, and even a little embarrassed, as she began to tell Kate about how sorry she was to have unloaded this burden on her the evening before.

"I want you to know, that I was caught a bit off guard by your question. I didn't want to lie to you about the photograph, and by the time I was through giving you the whole explanation about what happened, your father arrived to pick you up. I knew that you must have been shaken up just learning about all of this 'out of the blue' like that, and, well, I guess I just wanted you to know how terrible I felt about it after you left.

Please understand, Kate, it *was* a very tragic thing that I shared with you, but I *have* really managed to get through the toughest part. I guess that's why I felt I could finally talk about it with someone. I think you may have helped me over yet another hurdle in this long healing process because, being worried about you, I even got up the nerve to discuss the whole thing with your dad. He told me that you were pretty upset last night."

"Don't worry about me, Ms. Turner," Kate said in her most reassuring voice. "I cry during some of the T.V. commercials. I just felt awful about what happened to you. I had…, well, I just had no idea. But, really, don't worry about me."

With that, her dad came back out on the porch with lunch, and asked if he should come back in a little while.

After being assured by Jaycee Turner that it was very timely that he join them, he put the tray down on the table, poured three glasses of iced tea, told the ladies to help themselves and announced the 'sandwich du jour' as ham salad. Before anyone could even reach for one, though, it started pouring, and the rain was being blown all the way across the porch by gusts of wind that seemed to come from nowhere.

Kate managed to keep the sandwiches dry as she grabbed the tray and headed through the door with Jaycee and her dad close behind carrying the glasses of tea. All three managed to get only slightly wet in the hurried escape.

While they had lunch at the kitchen table, the storm came and went. This was typical of the occasional afternoon rains that rushed through these parts during the summer. But, although they usually lasted less than an hour, these passing storms often dumped a torrential kind of rain for a few minutes at a time, so even a dead run from the barn to the house would almost surely mean a total soaking.

When Jaycee brought up the subject of school beginning in just a few days she could sense, and even empathize with, Kate's lack of enthusiasm about it. She admitted to Kate that she had similar reservations about school as a teenager. She cautioned her, however, that since this was her senior year, the year that should offer lifelong kinds of memories, it would be a shame if she didn't find a way to savor the experience as much as possible.

"Speaking of school," remembered Jaycee, "I figured out what we should get done for your Physical Science course before we shift to meeting once a week. I think we should be right on schedule with one more session of two hours or so before school starts. I did confirm with Mr. Breen that as long as I submit your results by the first of October, the grade will be recorded in time for your college applications. Do you think we could get together sometime tomorrow? Maybe early afternoon?"

"Sure," answered Kate, without giving any thought to the meadow rendezvous she had agreed to only a couple of hours ago.

"Great, I'll come over and get you around 1:30 then," confirmed Ms. Turner.

With that, Michael began to clear the dishes from the table. Jaycee thanked him for his hospitality and made mention of how she now owed him *two* lunches. After assuring her that the pleasure was entirely mutual and that the lunches, in both cases, were more than earned, he told her that he hoped to do it again sometime.

This comment created an awkward silence for a moment while both Kate and Jaycee separately, and simultaneously, wondered if it was meant as a pleasant compliment or an open invitation for a date. Michael went about the job of wrapping the leftover sandwiches, quite oblivious to the question that he had unknowingly created.

"So, when did you plan to begin those riding lessons, Jaycee?" asked Kate's dad with a bit of a grin. As he said it he turned to Kate with a mischievous kind of look.

"Now?" Kate thought to herself as she returned his look with one of confusion.

"Well, I don't know. I guess I've been waiting for things to slow down a bit. With school opening in a few days, things will actually begin to settle back into an organized schedule for me. I sure have been thinking about it, though. Just watching Kate riding in today made me wish I had begun years ago," Jaycee lamented. "You just look so absolutely comfortable on that horse Kate."

"There's no time like the present for doing what you have put off for so long you know. Since you're already here, why don't you begin to collect on those lessons now? Look!" Michael pointed at the window. "The sun has broken through. The time seems right, doesn't it?" he pressed.

Realizing that her dad had obviously decided that this was to be the time to introduce Ms. Turner to her new horse, Kate joined in and let her know that Sanchez was still saddled, so all they would need to do is get another horse ready.

As much as she was thrilled with bartering the lessons when they had lunch together at the Big Sky Diner, and was absolutely committed to finally learning to ride, Jaycee hadn't really given any thought to when she might actually begin. It had been such a busy summer that it hadn't even crossed her mind, until today, when she watched Kate riding across the field toward the house, looking so carefree and natural.

She followed Kate and Michael across the long dirt driveway, somewhat tentative but mostly excited, stopping to admire the distinctive Pinto markings on Sanchez as they entered the barn. She stroked his neck while he stared at her as if he expected an introduction of some kind.

While Sanchez and Jaycee made friends, Kate and Michael went into the stall to get Duchess and walked her out to the tie-up. The sun streaming through the barn doors made her black skin shine as though she were wet, and when Jaycee turned back to see what was going on behind her, the image of this beautiful animal took her by surprise.

"Oh my! What a gorgeous horse!" she uttered. "Who is this? This can't be the horse *I'll* be riding, can it?"

"This is Duchess," Kate answered.

Sanchez, meanwhile, turned his head back and forth a couple of times as a signal that *he* wasn't quite ready to give up the attention. Not at all used to being shunned for a newcomer in his own barn, he seemed a bit confounded as Jaycee walked straight over to Duchess and began to rub her along the withers. As if he couldn't bear to watch, he turned completely around and looked the other way.

"Oh don't get jealous, big guy!" Kate consoled Sanchez as he hung his head. "Duchess just wants to meet her new owner."

"Duchess, is it? Well, Duchess, you are just… New owner?" Jaycee spun back toward Kate. "She *can't* be for sale?" she asked with her head nodding as though she was answering her own question

Kate and her dad looked at one another, each wondering if the other was going to answer.

"Well, Jaycee, not exactly. I mean she's not really for sale," Kate's dad began.

"I wouldn't think so. I can't imagine someone selling a horse like this. She is just *so* beautiful," Jaycee responded.

"What I mean is, not for *sale* actually. But, well, Kate and I thought you might like to have her," he said as Kate stood there with a huge grin.

There was a pause while the bewildered Jaycee glanced back and forth at Kate and her dad trying to understand exactly what was going on.

"*Have* her? You *can't* mean have her…. I mean…. That's crazy. Why would…?"

Kate jumped in at that point with the story about how they went down to get Duchess the prior weekend from the woman moving back east, and how she wanted to make sure the horse was cared for.

"When we had lunch at the 'Big Sky' you mentioned that you hoped to get a horse one day," Michael explained. "And when we saw Duchess here, and realized how well mannered she was, we figured she might be perfect for you."

Jaycee turned to look at the horse again. Almost half a minute passed without a word being spoken as she stood there, motionless, staring at Duchess.

"If this was a bad idea, or the timing isn't right for you, please don't be afraid to tell us, Jaycee," Michael recanted, suddenly concerned that the gesture was not taken well. "Kate is only too happy to keep the horse here for you. But, if you think this is a little premature, we understand completely."

"No, Michael," she paused. "As a matter of fact the timing is perfect. It is the best idea I've heard in a long, long time, and I'm really sorry for reacting this way. I just don't know what to think. I'm so shocked, I mean, my God! Look at her! I just can't believe you people thought of me when she was offered to you. I…, well, no one has ever done anything like this for me. You can't know how excited I am………. how grateful I am. There's no way for me to…..Thank you so much," she said standing there, somewhat awkward in the moment.

Exercising the privilege of youth, Kate broke the uncomfortable standoff by walking over and putting her arms around Jaycee for a sincere hug. She told her how happy she was for her, and for Duchess, to fall right into the hands of someone who would probably love her as much as her former owner.

It may have been because both the giving and receiving of truly meaningful things are equally rewarding. Or, it could have been the combination of Kate, having grown up lacking the influence of a woman, and Jaycee living with so much pain for so long that caused this spontaneous moment of affection to seem like one of those more memorable 'connections' in life, the kind that are unexplainable in the process, and unforgettable in the aftermath. Whatever the personal experiences that brought them to this moment, the bond that had been developing in these few short weeks was clearly galvanized in this exchange.

At her father's suggestion, Kate saddled Duchess for Jaycee to see how the horse would react to a different rider. She explained that some horses, having been used to one rider, can be very skittish about the change. After getting her ready, she led her out of the barn and helped Jaycee into the stirrup to hoist herself up. Duchess stood there as if everything was normal so, climbing aboard Sanchez, Kate started out of the barn with Duchess and Jaycee in tow, through the freshly made puddles of mud in the driveway and across the yard to the field for a leisurely stroll. Within a few minutes she could see that Duchess wasn't about to act up, so she brought her alongside and slid the reigns back over her neck to Jaycee.

As they walked, Jaycee began to philosophize about how strange it was that life could be almost ignored sometimes when people get so busy that they don't really stop to enjoy anything. She realized, and admitted, that she had been maintaining that kind of pace herself. But, riding through that field, on that beautiful horse, she told Kate that she was feeling different somehow, and that, little by little, she was beginning to appreciate life again.

When they returned and Kate finished showing her how to unbridle, unsaddle and brush down the Duchess, Jaycee remembered one of the reasons she had come.

"I know this is going to seem a very strange coincidence now," she announced as Michael was coming out of the house toward the two of them by the corral, "but I actually brought a gift with me which is for the two of you. I'm afraid, unfortunately, it won't seem like much now, in comparison to *your* incredible surprise. But, when I left the house I thought it was a pretty neat idea."

Jaycee walked to her car and took a telescope from out of the trunk. It was the one she had told Kate about, the one she received from her father upon graduating from college. Since buying the newer, more powerful model, she only kept it around for sentimental reasons. When Kate told her the story of her dad having used one so much when she was younger, she thought it might be of more use to the two of them than it would be collecting dust at her house.

"You remembered!" Kate exclaimed.

"Yes, I've been hanging on to this for no reason. I have another, so I thought you two might get some use out of it."

"The two of us, you say?" smiled Michael. "Apparently you two have been talking about the old days. I guess that must be what was behind our talk the other night," he said looking over at Kate.

Jaycee assured him that no family secrets were revealed, but just an explanation when she quizzed Kate about how she learned what she already knew about astronomy. She then suggested that since her gift was woefully shy of the kindness shown to her today, and since they still had to settle the boarding arrangement, they should allow her to treat them both to dinner.

Kate and her dad looked at one another, and simultaneously confessed to having made no plans. Since it was his turn to cook, Michael accepted the offer on behalf of both. They agreed to meet at the Big Sky at 6:30.

Each string resonated,
while every word conveyed his story,
in a melody I still carry.

Chapter Six

Music

Upon returning home later that evening, following a very pleasant dinner with Jaycee Turner, Kate decided to relax in her room for the rest of the night. She wanted to call Mal to tell her about the stranger she met, and she knew it could turn out to be a long conversation, so she got showered and into her pajamas before making the call.

Within the first two minutes on the phone, Mal, the one Kate considered to be the carefree Bohemian type, was actually preaching to her about the insanity of being in such close proximity to a total stranger out in the middle of nowhere. Mal was obviously taken aback by the sudden reversal of the common sense approach that she had come to expect from her predictable friend. After all, it had become her role to be the stable one in the relationship. But Kate explained, as best she could, that there was something about this guy, and there was no way she could resist the need she felt to know more about him.

"I have a feeling about this guy, Mal. I know it's weird, but I trust him. It's not even a question about danger. I absolutely know that he means no harm. But, somehow, it's like I know him. Not like he's familiar or anything but, I don't know, I guess it's just that I'm not used to meeting someone who is so different. Anyway, if you're worried about me, why don't you come along tomorrow? I'd love for you to meet him."

Mal sounded distraught while apologizing about not being able to go along. She had already promised her father that she would help set up the church hall for the quarterly 'Ham & Bean Supper', which diverted the conversation momentarily for some humorous reminiscing about the many times they worked that same detail together.

Before hanging up, Mal pleaded with her to wait until the following day to go, but Kate refused. Even if it wasn't for the fact that she had already promised to meet him the next day, she was much too anxious to find out more about him to wait longer anyway.

"Kate, if I didn't know any better I'd swear you have a thing for this guy, and that really scares me. You are supposed to be the stable one in this relationship. You can't just go changing into some reckless person now."

"Actually Mal," she contested, "I think it might be my turn. But, don't worry. This isn't as reckless as you are imagining it to be. This guy is not some serial killer. Now that I think of it, though, if you don't hear from me tomorrow night, will you tell someone where to look for me?"

"Oh, now that's funny! That's really a scream, Kate. How about I threaten to let your dad know where you're going. Would that be considered good humor? Would you stay home tomorrow then?"

"With all the stuff I could tell your folks?" Kate said jokingly. "C'mon Mal, give me some credit. If I thought there was any real danger here, you know I wouldn't go. Besides, Sanchez likes him, how bad could he be?"

"Excellent Kate!" Mallory sarcastically quipped. "Remind me to put your horse down as a character reference on my college application. I had no idea he had such credibility."

Mal's defection to the side of common sense could not have been predicted. By the time Kate realized that her own volley of heartfelt intuition was landing well short of the target, Mal was battering Kate's defensive position with the big guns of logic.

The argument obviously lost at this point, Kate decided that slipping away from the skirmish appeared to be the wiser strategy, so she attempted to escape the conversation with "I'll tell you what, Mal. I'll call you tomorrow night and give you the details, I promise."

"Oh, you'll be calling me all right!" Mallory emphasized. "I should be home no later than 8:00. Call me at exactly eight, and every five minutes after if I'm not here yet. Understood, friend of mine?"

"Okay, okay. I'll talk to you then. I promise. I'm going to bed now. Goodnight Mal!"

Hearing her best friend say, "Goodnight you reckless fool" before hanging up made Kate smile as she turned out the light for the night. The conversation made her think a bit before she went to sleep, about the unexpected turns in life that suddenly manage to occupy such a big percentage of attention when they occur. She was thinking how just a couple of weeks before life seemed absolutely boring, and the feeling of dread about summer school hung over her like so much extra weight. Then, unexplainably, the next day couldn't come fast enough. "Mallory, calling *me* a reckless fool," she thought before dozing off. "Now that's rich!"

The thin, lace curtains on the bedroom window told the story as Kate woke up. They were perfectly still. The clock radio read 6:33, and at this time of day, she thought, there should be a breeze, that night to day transitional kind of stirring in the air. But, the fact that it was perfectly still was a sure indication that the day's temperature was almost certain to be oppressive.

There was reason to be optimistic, though, it was a St. Cloud day.

By the time she made it through the shower, dressed, and lumbered downstairs there was a toasted English muffin and an orange juice already at the table awaiting her arrival. She no sooner sat down when her dad came into the kitchen and gave her a goodbye kiss on the cheek and told her he would be home around 3:00. As he walked out the door, he told her to make sure and shut off the coffee pot when she was through with breakfast, and wished her a nice day.

She passed on the muffin and sat enjoying some coffee while looking out on the yard through the patio doors. She realized there would be precious few mornings she could laze around like this. School would begin in just two days, and school mornings tended to be pretty hectic. It suddenly occurred to her that the addition of Duchess in the barn meant even more work before heading off to school, which translated to an even earlier waking time every morning. Reflecting back to the day before, though, at how happy they had made Jaycee, it still seemed well worth it, and she knew the extra money she would earn from the boarding would come in handy for something.

When Kate finally got motivated enough to get to her chores in the barn, it was a little later than her usual start time, and Sanchez's snorting was a clear indication that he was aware of the delay. Unfortunately, in order to get done and be on the trail in time for the rendezvous, it would now be impossible to make the grand picnic lunch she had planned. Mad at herself for having wasted too much of the morning, she rushed through the duties in the barn, got Sanchez saddled, and ran back into the house to throw together a lunch. After wrapping a couple of baloney sandwiches, grabbing the potato chips he had requested, rummaging through the cabinet for some kind of dessert, and putting two bottles of grape soda in a bag, she was ready to go.

Kate knew that it was awfully warm to be working poor Sanchez on an uphill climb in the mid-day sun. But, she decided it would be okay since it would get slightly cooler as they got to higher ground, and the return part of the trip would be downhill.

Much of the ride was spent thinking about the courage it must take for someone to head out to see the country, alone. She hadn't given it any serious thought before, but just taking up residence in some old hunting cabin in the middle of nowhere, which probably didn't even have electricity, was a tad more gutsy than she figured she could ever be.

Just as they approached the path into the meadow, Kate pulled Sanchez to a stop and remained still, listening because she thought she heard a noise. But, Sanchez didn't perk his ears as he normally would if there was any kind of an unidentified sound.

As she listened more intently, the sound became slightly more audible, and as they moved slowly along the path it was clear that it was music, and it was coming from the meadow. When she pulled Sanchez up again, he looked back with that one-eye look of bewilderment.

"Don't pretend you don't hear anything just because you're tired, boy!", she whispered. "If that was another animal I just bet it would be a different story, so you can just stop giving me that look."

At the end of the path, Kate could see across the field to her favorite reading spot, and there he sat, picking at a guitar. When he spotted her he leaned the guitar down against the felled tree and stood up to greet her with a smile and a wave.

As she approached he said; "I see my equine friend here brought you back."

"It was more my idea really," she jested as she made a quick dismount.

"Well," he chuckled, "*whoever* is responsible, I'm grateful. I was looking forward to continuing our discussion."

"So, you are saying that it's not the food you were looking forward to?"

"Of course not," he responded. "Wait!" he added. "I mean I'm saying yes, that it is *not* the food. Those double negative questions are always throwing me, although, I must say that the food *has* made more than a small contribution to my highlights here."

After Kate fitted the cuffs on Sanchez, she withdrew the lunch bag from his saddlebag and gave him the okay to go ahead and graze. While she put the bag on the ground by the tree and began taking out the contents, she wondered to herself how she was going to ask all the questions she hoped to get answered without making it sound like the third degree.

"What are those?" Elijah asked about the leg cuffs.

"These keep him from wandering off. A lesson learned with a long walk back home one day".

"He ran off?"

"Well," Kate explained, "more *walked away*, while I was napping".

"Huh. That's kind of funny," was Elijah's reaction.

"You're not the first to think so," Kate quipped as she sat down on the log. Opening the bag and handing her new friend a sandwich and drink, she asked him about his night in the wilderness.

"I absolutely love it up here," was his reply. "I only wish I could stay longer."

Kate told him how she came to find this place several years ago, when she first got Sanchez, and has been coming here to study, or just relax, ever since. She told him how surprised she was to know that someone else had been there. Although she said she knew deep down that there had to be many other people who had discovered this place, she had never seen any sign of anyone else having been there.

He was quick to agree that it was a beautiful place, and that he couldn't resist staying around a short time to enjoy it once he had happened by.

As she handed him a bag of chips, she suddenly thought back to his comment about wishing he could stay, and realized he made it sound as though he would soon be leaving.

"You're leaving?" she asked, trying to sound less than alarmed.

"Chips!", he said as though he had opened a Christmas present. "Thanks so much for remembering. This is really too much. Twinkies yesterday and chips today. I mean, it's really very gracious of you. I owe you, for sure."

"Well, you're a pretty easy guy to satisfy, I have to say. What did you say about leaving?"

Elijah explained that he needed to be somewhere before long to help someone out, and that he had a lot of distance to cover to get there. He told her that he had been taking his time traveling around thinking he had more of it, but that it was now important to get to where he was going as soon as possible.

"And how exactly do you plan to help this person, if you don't mind my asking?" Kate inquired.

"I can't say that I'm *exactly* sure," he confessed. "Guess I'll have to play that by ear."

"Where is it that you have to go?" she pried.

He employed the strategy of attempting to answer a different question as a dodge to her interrogation.

"Oh, I'm guessing it must be 1300 miles or so as the ol' raven flies, so I figure I really ought to get started tonight," he said with a coy grin on his face.

"Okay, sorry for the question," Kate offered, sensing his discomfort. "I really don't mean to pry. Anyway, it's 'as the crow flies', isn't it?"

"Crow, raven, I imagine the distance & routing to be pretty much the same for one blackbird as the other," he countered nonchalantly.

"Are you in some kind of trouble, like a fugitive or something, or do you just travel around helping people?" she asked sounding concerned as she took the cuffs off of Sanchez.

"I'm no Shao-lin priest, if that's what you hoped," he declared with a big smile.

"After all, I haven't helped you have I?"

Kate admitted that she didn't even know what a Shao-Lin priest was.

"Not much of a T.V. person, hey?" he seemed surprised. "I kind of thought with that 'Fugitive' reference, well, never mind, not important."

He assured her that he was really not in any trouble and tried to explain that there was good reason for not being totally open about his travel. He had decided that not answering was better than not telling the truth, so he confided that "Although it's not exactly the high ground, I hope you can accept that it *is* the way it has to be just now. Not for my sake, but I may end up having to help someone else out of trouble. Anyway, how about we talk about you again. Would that be okay?"

"Actually, no," Kate answered sounding disappointed. "I'm not totally satisfied with this mystery. But, I suppose the best I can hope for is that when you feel you can talk about it, you will let me know.

"Anyway, there's not much to tell." she reluctantly admitted after deciding to concede. "I'm sure my life would seem pretty boring compared to someone who travels around the country on their own."

"No, I doubt that. What about plans for the future? Family? How do you do in school? A boyfriend? Yeah, tell me about the fortunate son that gets to take Miss Kate to the big dance?" he asked as though she were the most popular girl in school.

"Well, if you mean the Prom, no one is beating the door down yet, but I have several long months of school to get through before I have to concern myself with that." "No steady boyfriend? No love of your life?" he asked suspiciously.

"No steady. And the love of my life happens to belong to someone else," she sheepishly admitted.

"Oh, my! Then you really *are* talking to the right guy."

"Why is that? Are you going to come back from your secret adventure and take me to the Prom?" she quipped.

"Actually, I meant that I could relate to the kind of situation in which you find yourself. I can tell you a story about unrequited love."

Kate smiled and said, "Well, misery loves company. I'm listening."

"This happens to be a story of a kid that doesn't really find his way into the popular circles in any of the many schools he attends, but the love of his high school days is definitely in that group. Of course, she doesn't notice him because she focuses her affection on the captain of the basketball team at the time," he lamented, stopping to think a moment before going on.

"Anyway, it turns out that he and Josephine go their separate ways, but he never forgets her." As Elijah reaches back to pull the guitar onto his lap, he tells Kate of a song that was written, as a matter of fact, on Prom night, after having caught a glimpse of her "all done up in this navy blue sequined dress with white gloves and pearls. It was one of those memorable visions," he said as he started fingering the strings in stops and starts, as though he were trying to remember a forgotten tune. The notes fell into a slow, sad sounding rhythm in only a few moments, and he played for more than a minute before starting to sing;

"She's seventeen going on twenty,

with the moves of a fashion queen.

Such a beautiful face, such elegant grace,

this girl, this woman, Josephine.

Josephine I know I'm crazy.

But I'm crazy for the beauty unseen,

while the rest see your style, your magazine smile,

I see the girl, the woman, Josephine

"Wow, I haven't thought about that song for sometime. It's funny what you carry with you."

Kate's attention was drawn to his fingers as they slowed to the end of their recital, several seconds after he stopped talking. They seemed to be resonating notes in harmony with her nerve endings. Those few bars, in that setting, on such a beautiful day, well, she was suddenly very glad that she didn't let Mallory talk her out of being there.

"Sounds like Josephine missed out," she said in what somehow came out as not much more than a whisper.

"I guess we never get to know about those things," he said as if he was quite all right with it. "Who knows?

"I am a believer, though, that there must be certain connections that exist here. Things which we don't understand, connecting one person to another," he explained. "I mean, there are all these incredible forces at work in all of the universe, like moons being held to planets, planets to stars, and stars sometimes to one another, all held within galaxies. It would seem naïve to me to think that there wouldn't be similar kinds of bonds existing between the people walking around on one of these spheres. How else could we explain things like meeting someone for the first time and feeling like we already know them? Or two people having so much in common they seem like twins?

"As a matter of fact, I have this feeling that we are bound, at some point in our existence, to cross paths with those with whom we share these *bonds*; kind of like the way a comet might disappear from our sight for long periods of time, its course still determined, you know, and bound to eventually return.

"Now, the trick with all this, at least I *think* the trick with all this, comes in recognizing these connections when they occur. I can't help but get the feeling that we tend to walk by them more often than not. Don't you think so?

"God, I'm sorry *again*, I got sidetracked here somehow. I'm sure I was trying to make an important point along the way, but I can't tell you exactly what it was. Can you?"

While Elijah shook his head in recognition that he went way past the point he probably would have liked to end this rambling, Kate was making the assumption that both questions were rhetorical, but the awkward silence that followed made it seem like there was an answer of some kind expected.

She was temporarily sidetracked herself, however, wondering if he was implying anything about him and her in all this talk about "connections." Even though she was quick to disregard even the possibility of such speculation, it was exactly what she had been trying to describe to Mallory. That there was a sort of connection to him. Suddenly the thought of his leaving without her getting to know him better seemed wrong. It was painfully clear to her that this could only be righted by either making him stay or knowing more about him.

"Why don't you trust me to know who you are, or where you're really going?" she blurted out, not even believing she said it.

With a look of surprise, Elijah turned to face her.

"Well, *there's* some ground I had hoped we already covered." Pausing just long enough for Kate to wish she hadn't asked the question, he continued; "As a matter of fact, Kate, even having known you for this short time, I think I do trust you. But, this has nothing to do with trust. It is a simple matter of helping someone that may be in some trouble by the time I get there and, who knows, by association I may be in some kind of trouble before it's done. I just don't see any purpose for you knowing anything more about me *or* him, at least at this point in time.

"I guess *you* will have to be the one to trust *me* this time," he said as he looked straight into her eyes.

"I've got to tell you, Just Elijah," she said returning his stare, "I don't know *why* I trust you, but for some reason, I guess I do. Maybe it's because you're the only one I know that likes Twinkies besides my dad, or that Sanchez seems to like you. I don't know. My best friend thinks I'm insane for even talking to you." After a pause she continued, "I guess I just feel that if this turns out to already be goodbye, I can't help but wish I knew more about you, that's all."

"Your friend is only looking out for you, I'm sure. But, you have a keen sense for people and you will probably do well if you follow your instincts more. Believe me, I do appreciate your trust in me. You have to know that disappointing you is not something I would intentionally do.

"What if I promise to see you again when I come back this way? Maybe by then I can tell you more. How would that be?"

Kate, visibly perked up with the prospect of seeing him again, was able to partially mask her excitement by turning her back to mount Sanchez. Making her best effort to appear slightly less enthusiastic than she really felt about his offer, so as not to appear the starry eyed schoolgirl, she casually answered "First of all, mystery man, I'm not disappointed, just curious. Secondly, if you *do* happen back this way. I really *would* like to hear about the rest of this adventure of yours."

"Then I'll just do it. I'll come back this way," he said, looking skyward as though he was counting in his head. "Let's say four or five weeks from now, at the most. How would that be? I could meet you right here five weeks from today."

"I'll shake on that," Kate leaned down from the saddle offering her hand. "In the meanwhile, I wish you safe travels. And, I really do hope that you are able to help this friend of yours."

With that, she and Sanchez were heading back toward the opening to the trail. She turned once as she got to the edge of the path, and saw that he was sitting back down watching her leave. There was a twinge of temptation to ride back and ask him, again, not to go. But, somehow the prospect of not seeing him again was, although sad, not tragic. He had blown in and out of her life like a summer storm, with no real damage, but some very welcome relief from an otherwise boring time.

Kate was really glad she had met him, and along the quiet trail she gave some thought to what he had said about connections between people, and how odd it was that their paths had crossed at all. In the short time spent with him, she knew that he would make a great friend, maybe even a boyfriend, if he stayed. She got more insight from him in two brief meetings than from all the advice she had gotten during the entire summer from Mallory.

But, she would try not to allow herself to get excited about the possibility of his return. His promise, she suspected, was probably just a way of making the leaving easier. If he did, she would truly love to see him again and hear about the rest of his journey, and if he didn't, she was sure she would not forget him any time soon.

While Kate was gone her father had driven to the market to get a few things they needed. He was never one for doing a "grocery binge" which is what he called getting a two week supply of everything. He didn't mind the stop every other day. He had explained on several occasions to Kate that his feeling was he would have to stop regularly for fresh bread, which he thought should accompany every meal, and fresh vegetables anyway. "Besides," he told her so many times, "how would I know what I would want to eat next week."

He saw Jaycee's Mustang as he searched for a place to park in the supermarket lot, and pulled in next to it.

While he was busy trying to find the right elements for the salad he planned that evening, he did not notice her come up behind him until she tapped him on the back.

"A man buying romaine lettuce?" she teased with a sly voice. "Now I'm *really* impressed!"

"Well hi! How are you, Jaycee? Is that what this is?" he smiled.

After exchanging the standard greeting, and saying they each were fine, Michael confessed to her that, although he had plenty of practice, he still didn't consider himself much of a cook.

"Well, you know what then, Michael?" she told him as she pointed her finger so it was touching his chest. "I'm going to make you a heck of a dinner. I owe you a lot, so I won't take no for an answer. Just tell me when will it be?"

He was at a loss for words, and could only nod in agreement before she repeated the part about committing to a time.

"What about the day after tomorrow?" she pressed.

"Great. Sure. But you don't really….."

"Good!" she said to interrupt his "that's not necessary" speech. "I'll call you about the time. Good luck with the produce!" she grinned as she pushed her cart away.

"And just like that," he thought to himself on the way home, "we have a *date?*"

"What becomes of the little boys,
who never comb their hair?
They're lined up all around the block,
on the Nickel, over there."

Tom Waites

Chapter Seven

Art

In many parts of the Midwest, the distance one can see while standing at ground level is often dependent upon the season, and how high the corn is. Once the final cutting takes place, the flatter areas expose panoramic views with only sparse interruptions of hardwoods or man made structures. The scenery offered in these broad expanses would not be considered majestic by most, but like all of nature, there are those moments.

A certain haunting beauty comes about when the longer shadows of September lay across these wide open fields, and the livestock seem to bask in the waning glow as if preparing for the "oppressive" slant of light that Emily Dickinson describes of "winter afternoons" to come.

On occasion, just prior to twilight, the plowed acreage can take on an eerie resemblance to a deserted battlefield as the green and yellow equipment sits idle in the dirt like so much broken artillery. But, it is only when the crows begin to resemble penguins, as they waddle over the evenly humped rows, that one comes to realize that 'still life' is an art form best enjoyed without extensive staring.

It was on just this sort of clear September evening that young Jack Taylor sat on the sprawling porch of the General Store gazing down the two-lane road that led into town. Jack was watching a figure off in the distance as it made its way along the road that ran perpendicular to the one leading to the store. He was able to determine that it was definitely someone walking, but it was too far off to tell much more than that.

Jack would sit on this same porch from time to time watching cars coming along that same road. He usually made a game of trying to guess whether the car would turn onto the road to the store or keep going straight into the next town. Since most cars, he learned by experience, did not come up the road that went by the store, it was a bit more of a gamble to guess in favor of that option. Sometimes, even at that distance, Jack would recognize the car, which made the guess a lot easier. But, usually he just relied on things like how fast the car was going (There was a cut-off point after which the guess would no longer count because the car would have to begin to slow for the turn around that point), and of course there was no guessing once the directional signal was seen.

Just as this particular pedestrian was about to reach the cut-off point, the one for cars, Jack made up his mind the person would definitely turn. It took another few minutes for the walker to make the intersection, but sure enough, a turn it was. Jack nodded his head and made the same all-knowing smirk that he made every time he guessed right with the cars.

Coming now straight toward the store, the figure was getting smaller as it approached the depression in the road between the store and the intersection. Once the figure reappeared and slowly began to get bigger, Jack became convinced that it had to be a man by the way he walked. And as he got closer, he could see that something was sticking up from his shoulder. "Gotta be a hunter with a rifle," he thought, not realizing that hunting season didn't actually begin for several weeks.

Jack was standing at the rail when the walker finally reached the stairs of the store. They stood about fifteen feet apart staring at one another for a few moments before the man spoke.

"Do you suppose it would be okay if I got some water out of the faucet there?" he asked, pointing to the wall on the side of the store.

"I think it's okay, Mister," Jack answered.

"Much appreciated, and I prefer Elijah," stated the stranger as he pulled the guitar and bedroll off his back. "Been too long without a ride on that road, and I'm more than a little thirsty."

"Would you like a root beer?" Jack offered. "I've got twenty cents left, and Mrs. Wheaton usually lets me have 'em for twenty cents."

"As much as it would be hard for me to think of a bigger treat right at this moment, I couldn't possibly take your money there, young man, but I am very grateful for the offer," Elijah said as he turned on the faucet. "I can be more than satisfied with some of this water."

"Junior? Don't go playing with that water now!" came from inside the store a few moments after Elijah turned on the faucet.

"It's not me, Mrs. Wheaton. I told this man he could use some of your water. He's thirsty," Jack yelled back.

"Okay! That's fine. Just make sure you shut it off tight when you're done," shouted the woman inside.

"We will!" Jack promised.

While Elijah was pouring water into his hands and splashing it on his face and over the back of his neck, Jack went inside. When he came back out, he looked around and didn't see anyone. Walking to the end of the porch, he could see Elijah sitting down, leaning against the shade tree toward the back of the store. His eyes were closed and his hair was dripping down his face onto his shirt.

"Here's your root beer," Jack said softly as if waking him from a nap.

"Junior, is it?" asked the stranger, with one eye open.

"Not really. Mrs Wheaton is the only one that calls me that. My name is Jack Taylor," the boy responded.

"Well, Jack Taylor," Elijah announced. "It's a very generous thing you did, spending your last twenty cents on me like this. I want you to know I appreciate your kindness." After taking a long sip from the frosty bottle, and keeping it in his mouth for an extended time while making the 'MMmmmm' sound, Elijah swallowed the drink, smiled, and leaned back against the tree again.

Seeing how grateful the man seemed to be made Jack feel quite proud of the gesture.

"Is this what you do all day, Jack? Greet people coming into town? Because I've gotta tell ya, if everybody around here is as friendly as you, I might just have to stay here awhile."

"No", Jack said with a big grin, "after school I help sweep out the store and the porch everyday. Mrs. Wheaton gives me forty-five cents for that. But, I already spent twenty-five cents of it on some baseball cards before you came."

"Get any good ones with that 25 cents?" the exhausted Elijah inquired as he took another sip and slid down to a more comfortable, more inclined position.

"I got mostly doubles, except for the Brewer's team card."

There was a slightly audible "Brewers?" from Elijah, which seemed to confirm the fact that he had heard the answer. But, either in the process of making that sound, or within a very few seconds following, he fell fast asleep against that tree.

Jack stood over his new friend like someone protecting a defenseless animal. After several minutes went by, he wasn't sure what he should do. He knew it was just beginning to get dark, which meant it was time to be going home, but he wasn't about to leave Elijah just lying there, alone in the dark.

"Mister?" he whispered as he bent down to be closer to Elijah's ear.

"Mister!" he called again in a slightly heavier whisper. "Are you okay? Are you gonna sleep right here tonight?"

With one eye reopened, Elijah acknowledged that he was both awake and okay, and apologized for having rudely fallen off in the middle of their conversation.

"Did I miss anything, Jack?" he asked, mid-stretch. "By the way, do you call everyone older than you 'Mister'?"

Sitting up straight now, rubbing his face with his hands as if he was washing himself, Elijah explained that he was so tired because he couldn't get many rides along the back roads he was taking, so he ended up walking most of the day. He told him that it was such a beautiful night he was thinking of just sleeping under the stars somewhere nearby.

"I can hear coyotes out here from my bedroom window at night," the suddenly wide- eyed Jack presented as heartfelt evidence that sleeping under the stars was a scary proposition.

"Well, Jack," Elijah responded looking equally concerned, "In that case, I believe I'll look at one of these barns, and some nice soft hay, for a good night's sleep then. As a matter of fact, before I doze off right here again, I think I'll start that search right now. I suppose you need to be getting home before long anyway, yes?"

"Yeah, I guess," was all Jack said as he turned around to start walking home. He took only a couple of steps when he turned back with a sort of dejected look and asked,

"Will you still be here tomorrow, Mister?"

"Well, I don't think I have the energy to head out tomorrow, Jack, so I'm thinking I might just hang around here for the day." Elijah answered. "What time do you get out of school tomorrow anyway?"

"Tomorrow is Saturday, Sir, I don't have school."

"Saturday, right!" Elijah acknowledged with some surprise. "Well then, why don't we get together sometime tomorrow, Jack, and you can show me some of your other baseball cards. Maybe we can swap a few of those doubles."

"You got cards?" Jack beamed.

"I've still got a few of my favorites," Elijah confirmed. "I'll tell you what. You meet me here at the store tomorrow, after you have your breakfast, and I'll show you. Right now though, you probably ought to be getting on home, don't you think?"

"Okay then, I'll see ya tomorrow," the boy agreed excitedly, raising his arm in the air in a fumbled combination of a wave and a salute as he turned again for home. "Have a good sleep, Mister Elijah!" he called out as he walked away, leaving his new friend sitting there on the ground smiling in the twilight.

"Goodnight there, Mister Jack," he mouthed too softly for the now running boy to hear.

Breakfast time during the weekends at the Gilchrest home was not Jack's favorite part of the day. Mr. Gilchrest, his Foster father, worked in a factory in Kokomo during the week, so he was always gone before Jack got up. But, on the weekend he was home all day, and he got up real early anyway, just to get a head start, Jack thought, on getting into a bad mood. By the time the family got together for breakfast, and he insisted the family eat breakfast together every Saturday and Sunday, he was always in a bad mood about how hard he had worked all week, or how far he had to drive to get to work everyday, or how much trouble he was having with the car, or something. One thing was sure, every weekend, almost without fail, Mrs. Gilchrest was going to end up crying about something Mr. Gilchrest didn't like.

The best that Jack could hope for on this particular Saturday, as he got dressed in his room, was that he didn't get assigned to any unexpected chores. That's what typically happened if Mr. Gilchrest got real mad. He would start yelling at Jack, complaining all the while about how the State didn't give him enough money to cover what it cost to keep a Foster child, or because he felt Jack didn't do enough to "earn his keep". When this happened, it almost always resulted in Jack having to stack wood, or rake the yard, or whatever chore popped into Mr. Gilchrest's mind at the time. But it was always an immediate assignment, and Jack couldn't afford that today, not if he was going to meet Elijah right after breakfast.

Every once in a while Mr. Gilchrest had to work on Saturday. "Overtime for the blood-suckers" was how he would refer to the extra workday. 'Holiday' was the description Jack adopted and, although Mrs. Gilchrest would never discuss it, he was sure she would agree with his sentiment.

When Jack turned the corner at the end of the hall and entered the kitchen, the chair that Mr. Gilchrest always sat in was empty, and Mrs. Gilchrest said a cheerful, "Good morning, young man!" That tone in her voice was usually only heard on school mornings, when Mr. Gilchrest wasn't home, which could only mean that it must be an 'overtime' day.

"What luck!" Jack thought to himself.

It was only corn flakes and a piece of toast, but it was the peaceful humming of Mrs. Gilchrest as she stood by the sink peeling apples that made it the most enjoyable meal he had eaten in awhile. When he was finished, he brought his bowl to the sink where she was standing and hugged her around the waist. It was an unspoken acknowledgment that he knew she was enjoying this particular morning for the same reason he was. She ran her fingers through his thick black hair as if to comb it back, smiled when he looked up at her, and said, "You go out and enjoy the day, dear! I've got lots to get done around here."

With that he raced back to his room to get the shoe box full of cards, put a rubber band around it so the top wouldn't come off, and headed out the front door shouting, "I'll be down at the store, Mrs. Gilchrest," behind him as he left.

Between Jack's house and the store was a little more than a quarter mile of straight road, with the halfway point marked by the huge barn at the Favreau farm. This was one of the biggest farms in town. Mr. Favreau had three silos to store the corn for his cows in the winter. Jack stood in one of those silos during the past summer, and it was too hard for him to even imagine how much corn could fit in there when it was filled. Mr. Favreau explained to him once that cows had to eat a lot in the winter to keep warm.

As Jack was walking past the farm, he noticed something sticking up out of the hay wagon, which was parked by the side of the barn. As he got closer, he thought it looked like the top of a guitar, like the one that he saw sticking up from Elijah's shoulder as he walked toward him the day before.

Veering from the road onto the grass, he slipped through the middle strands of the barbed wire fence to approach the wagon. Jack could see that it was definitely the top of a guitar once he got within about twenty feet. When he got up to the end of the wagon to take a closer look, he eyed Elijah emerging from behind the barn.

"Hey Mister!" he called out. "It's me, Jack."

Elijah signaled him with an index finger to his lips, the universal sign for silence, as he walked along the barn toward him.

When he got close enough he said, in little more than a whisper; "I'm trying to keep a kind of low profile here, Jack. I never really asked permission to sleep in their hay wagon or use the water this morning."

"It's okay, Mr. Favreau won't mind if he knows you're a friend of mine. I help him sometimes. He's real nice," Jack assured him. "Anyway, he doesn't come around the barn after the cows go out in the morning, unless it's raining."

"Well, in that case, hop up to my temporary living quarters," grinned Elijah, pointing at the hay wagon. "It's plenty comfortable on that loose hay, so what do you say we sit right here, look at those cards, and enjoy the morning sun?"

"Sure!" Jack agreed. Tossing his shoebox up first, he then hopped up onto the end of the wagon and sat back against the side. After smoothing the hay out behind him to get comfortable, Jack pulled the rubber band off the decorated shoebox, lifted the cover and proudly held out the seven hundred and sixteen cards he owned for Elijah to see.

"That's a lot of cards, Jack! Let's see what you've got there."

Gently taking the box and placing it on his lap, Elijah began leafing through the cards from the front of the box to the back. For more than an hour he pulled one card out after another and studied it while Jack made comments either about the player or how he acquired the card.

"I haven't kept up with this for awhile, so some of these I'm not familiar with, but I see you've got some classics here too."

"Yeah, my dad gave me a few that he saved from when he was a kid. He had lots more, but when he died I don't know what happened to them."

"I'm sorry to hear about that, Jack. You live with your mother now?" asked Elijah.

"No, she died too. I live with the Gilchrests now," Jack said while pointing toward his house. In a voice of casual resignation, he went on to explain "Pete was living with them when I got here, but he got adopted before the summer. I think probably no one will adopt me because of the fire. But I guess I don't care. I don't really want to go live with another family I don't even know."

Between the memories of his own loneliness as a child, and the helpless feeling that comes with knowing that any child has had to experience what Jack just described, Elijah was drawn to reflect for a moment, staring at Jack without speaking.

"You want to walk over to the pond and feed the fish?" said Jack in order to break the silence. "There's some huge fish in the pond."

"Well, that sounds pretty good." Elijah said somewhat hesitant.

"I was wondering, though, what sort of eating establishments there might be in this area. Any good places for a guy to get breakfast?"

"Yeah, there's a really good place for breakfast down the road that way." Jack pointed the opposite direction of the way Elijah came into town. "It's called Lou's Diner".

"Maybe I should walk down and have Lou make me a nice hot breakfast then, and come back to see your pond right after. I think this morning sun is reaching the end of the pleasant stage anyway." Sensing some disappointment on Jack's face, Elijah invited him to go along, but Jack admitted he already had breakfast.

"No thanks. I can't go. And Lou isn't there any more. There's only two Tommys there now. Big Tommy always makes Mr. Gilchrest laugh, except when he's really busy. If he's really busy he says 'no show today'.

"Hey! What about we stop at my house instead. It's right on the way to the pond, and I can grab some cookies that Mrs Gilchrest was taking out of the oven when I left, and I could even make a sandwich if you want one. She always has stuff for sandwiches. If you're still hungry after that, you could try to hitch a ride over to 'Koral Hamburg'. Everybody says they have the best cheeseburgs in the state."

"Cheeseburgs huh? Well, if you really think that Mrs Gilchrest wouldn't mind, the fresh cookies sound even better than 'Two Tommy's'. Lead on!" he said as he replaced the cover on the box of cards and put the rubber band around it. Once Jack jumped down from the wagon Elijah handed him the box, telling him he wanted to look at the rest of them when they got to the pond. He collected his guitar and bedroll and climbed down over the side of the wagon.

On the way past his house, Jack ran in to get the snacks and some bread for the fish while Elijah waited in the shade of the big tree across the road. As he sat back against the tree, his attention was drawn to the detail of the collage that decorated the shoebox full of cards in his lap. Every inch of each side of the box was covered with words or pictures apparently cut out of magazines and newspapers. The top was covered with faces or poses of baseball players, none of which Elijah recognized, and a team picture of the Chicago White Sox. One of the long sides was covered with a variety of cars and animals, while the other sported the word JACK in big letters, each letter distinctly different in color and design.

On one end of the box was a somewhat faded photograph of a young couple. Under the photo was taped a part of a white page with small print that appeared to be a page torn out of a book. As he read the excerpt, Elijah could feel the pain of the boy that felt it special enough to save.

Not Home

*When those ghosts come stalking in the middle
of the night,*

*can you cry out for your parents, to come and
hold you tight?*

*Or do you have to beg the staff to leave the
door ajar for light,*

*while you lay your head back on the bed and
pray to ease the fright?*

*Will someone hold your hand to make the
darkness seem all right?*

*Or has the lady in the hall gone and
wandered out of sight?*

*Do you try to keep from sleeping and resist with
all your might,*

*when those ghosts come stalking in the middle
of the night?*

Elijah, once again reminded of his own memories of living in a state facility, began to read the verse a second time when Jack came running out of his house carrying a paper sack shouting, "I made peanut butter sandwiches for a picnic."

Elijah, fashioning a convincing smile, said, "Now there's an idea," as Jack got close enough to hear. Working his way to a standing position, Elijah put his hand on Jack's shoulder and told him that he couldn't think of anything that sounded better than a picnic on such a beautiful day.

They walked, at a less than determined pace, about three quarters of a mile past Jack's house and turned off the road to a path that cut through a stand of hardwoods, which apparently grew up around the natural spring, which Jack called "the pond". The path was covered with poplar leaves of mellow gold, and at the end of the path were several swamp maples, which were reflecting brilliant red in the sunlit water. As they came to the end of the natural trail, Elijah was finishing his explanation of what it was like to travel around on his own, in answer to Jack's curiosity.

The air turned noticeably cooler in the shade of the trees, and once by the edge of the small pond, Jack pointed out the spot where the fish could be seen. The few crumbs he tossed into the water floated for more than a minute before two skinny catfish swam lazily toward the shore and sucked them down from the surface. Jack was smiling as though he had just hand fed the killer whale at Sea World.

"That's Fred and Barney," he said, pointing at one and then the other.

"After the Flintstones?" Elijah acknowledged.

"No, the other Fred and Barney," mused the suddenly sharp-tongued, chortling tour guide.

"Okay. I deserved that one," Elijah laughed. "But people I've been talking to lately don't seem to watch TV. Rest assured, though, young wit, I'll be on my toes from this point," he grinned as he rubbed Jacks head enough to muss his hair.

Watching the feeding continue until the slice of bread was gone and the pet fish retreated to shaded water, and looking duly impressed the whole time, Elijah finally commented, "I must admit, Jack, as much as I have always missed the penchant for pet fish in some cheesy glass bowl, keeping them in the wild like this is definitely cool."

Proudly nodding his head in agreement, Jack began walking back toward the shade. "Would you like your sandwich now?" he asked as he picked out a grassy place to sit and began to empty the contents of the bag.

"I really am grateful, Jack," was the response as Elijah reached for the offering. "Such a beautiful day, a peaceful setting, good company *and* food! At the risk of catching another witty example of mid-western, pre-teen sarcasm, what more could anyone possibly ask?"

Smiling while contemplating the comment, Jack retrieved his own sandwich from the bag, and then stuck his hand back in to pull out a short stack of donut size cookies. Holding them up so Elijah could see, he told him Mrs. Gilchrest had just finished baking this batch when he ran in the house to get the bread, and that she insisted he take some along with his sandwiches. "She makes the best oatmeal raisin cookies I ever had," admitted Jack.

"Well, that caps it, Jack Taylor," announced Elijah as he took a bite of the sandwich. "This sandwich you made is on fresh baked bread, and you say she makes great cookies? You're just going to have to find out if these Gilchrest folks will take in someone my age," Elijah joked.

After a few minutes of silence while he enjoyed the sandwich, Elijah sensed that Jack had drifted off somewhere.

"It sounds like you have had it kind of rough for someone your age there, Jack. If you don't mind my asking, how exactly did you end up here anyway? And, what's the story with this fire you mentioned earlier?"

Jack explained how he came to be with the Gilchrests after being in a group home up in the city. He said he hated being there, so he was really excited about getting out to live with another family, especially when he was told that it would be in the country. He told Elijah about the family he lived with before the group home, and how he accidentally set fire to their shed when he was lighting a firecracker. So, he was sent to live at the Wyatt School which, he explained, was a state home for boys with behavior problems.

At the group home, they told him he needed to work on his "aggressive behavior", and that setting that fire was the way he expressed his anger, though he was always pretty sure it was just an accident.

"I had to go to school the whole summer that year, but," he explained, "I told them I wasn't even mad when I lit that fire-cracker. I just wanted to hear the noise. I guess it was too close to the cans of paint. I sure never meant for that shed to catch on fire. Anyway, if I did have any anger I suppose the medicine they gave me at the Wyatt School took care of that. It made me so tired all the time, I just wanted to stay in bed."

"Jeez Louise! You got a Whitey Ford card?" Elijah's surprise temporarily interrupted the story.

"Yeah," replied Jack. "That was one of my dad's."

"I didn't mean to interrupt, Jack. I want you to understand, by the way, that I spent most of *my* whole childhood in group homes and with Foster families, so I think I have a pretty good feeling for what you're talking about. I sure remember what it was like to feel alone in the world at your age. Tell me, though, after the home, you said you were excited about coming down here. How come it sounds like you're not so excited anymore?"

"I don't know. I guess I want to go back up to the city. I just don't like the way Mrs. Gilchrest is sad all the time because Mr. Gilchrest gets so mad. I think part of the reason he's so mad is 'cause Pete left. He was almost thirteen, and he was a lot bigger than me, so he always helped Mr. Gilchrest with the wood and stuff. He never really wants me to help him much. After Pete left, I heard Mr. Gilchrest tell Mrs. Gilchrest that 'the wrong one got taken'.

"Anyway, there's no one to play with around here. I see Robby on the school bus, but he lives a long way from here, and I don't have a bike to get there even if I *could* go over to his house sometimes.

"I've got a friend up near the city, though, from when I was in the regular school. He told me a long time ago that he was pretty sure he could talk his mom into letting me stay with them. He doesn't have a dad.

"I was thinking I might go and find him sometime. Probably no one would look for me there. His mom works at this place that made one of the big rides at Disneyworld. It's called 'Major Tool'. I know it because she gave me a baseball hat with the name on it when she took me & Deven there to see these huge machines, and I still have it."

When Elijah had finished looking through the cards he gave Jack a long stare.

"Why are you looking at me?" asked Jack.

"I was really young when I lost my folks," Elijah recounted. "As a matter of fact, I don't remember much about how it was living with them. But, I just knew back then that no matter where else I lived it couldn't be the same. I always felt that I got a raw deal.

"When I look back at my situation I guess I was looking for Ozzie and Harriet to come along and think that I was the greatest thing since sliced bread, attitude and all. And I'm sure the people I was sent to live with were not waiting their whole lives to meet a kid who already had a huge chip on his shoulder. It was a simple matter of looking at what I didn't have instead of what I did. I guess a little tolerance and understanding on my part might have gone a long way to make things easier back then. I think some of the people I lived with tried a lot harder to make it bearable than I did.

"Some folks, I think, become Foster parents, or even adopt kids, because they figure they have enough room in their homes to care for total strangers. Some, I think, even have enough room in their hearts. But, sometimes I guess it just doesn't turn out the way either side pictured it, not because of the kid, or because of the new family. Maybe the chemistry isn't right. Maybe they aren't prepared to love a kid that is too angry to love them back. Maybe the kid is too afraid to trust anyone. Whatever the reason, I know now that it is usually a tough situation for both."

"Well, I've only been with two families, and I know I screwed up the first time but, except for being bored, both times were better than living in the group home.

"Did you like living with families you didn't know better than living in a group home Mister?" Jack asked.

"I did. It was a bit closer to what I saw as a normal living. Made me feel more like other kids."

"It's not as scary," Jack added. "I hope I never have to go back, but I don't know if I can stay here 'til I'm grown up. Mrs. Gilchrest doesn't know either. I don't like it here, but it is better than the home."

"This is what I'm getting at, Jack. Maybe your situation can improve. Whether it is here, the home or another family.

"I have always remembered one of my social workers saying 'It's the irritation of the sand that causes the oyster to form the pearl'. But, it wasn't until much later that I saw the wisdom in that simple line."

Jack was sitting there listening to Elijah as though he were reading to him from a Batman comic. This was the first person who ever talked about being alone, and really knew about it. And it was the first time in a long time that an adult talked to him without making him feel as though it was a lecture. The kids he made friends with in the group home were usually more messed up than he was, and at least as afraid. But, the way Elijah talked about it made it seem like he was talking about his own life. He reached for piece after piece of the tall grass next to where he sat, and chewed on each while Elijah talked on.

"Now that I've had a few years to think about all that stuff behind me, I can tell you one thing I do know from the experience, Jack. In the end it's you who decides if it all becomes a reason to succeed, or an excuse to fail, and I truly believe that decision will come from how well you learn to focus on what you have instead of worrying about what you don't.

"You know, sometime during one of my stays at a group home, between Foster families, I came up with this idea that I could improve my chances of being happier with the next place I would be sent. I decided that I would be happy no matter what. So, when I was finally placed in another home, I began to put the extra effort into trying to make the situation as good as I could. 'Whatever it takes' became my motto.

"It's something you might want to consider, Jack

"As a matter of fact, I'd be willing to make you a little deal, my friend. If you promise me you won't do anything crazy, like take off for the city on your own, until after you have tried this out for awhile. Well, I'll give you my favorite classic card."

"What's your favorite card?" Jack asked.

"Well, I don't carry my all-time favorite one with me," Elijah answered, "but it's definitely the Ted Williams card, and I don't see one here," he acknowledged while looking down at the box.

"Yeah, I had one though," reflected Jack with a solemn face. "My dad liked Ted Williams a lot. He had one of his cards mounted in a frame in my room when I was small, one that was really hard to get he told me."

"Here's the deal, my young friend." Elijah explained. "You might want to try it the way I did for awhile, and just do whatever it takes to try to make things better here."

"Like what?" Jack seemed puzzled.

"Like I said," Elijah emphasized, "*whatever it takes*. If Mr. Gilchrest is happier when someone is helping out with the chores, show him that you're plenty capable of helping him, and he doesn't have to tell you when to do it. If Mrs. Gilchrest seems sad, try to cheer her up. If you're smiling, maybe it will catch on. You don't have to accept things as they are, Jack. Even if you don't end up changing anything, you'll save yourself a lot of second-guessing later by putting in the effort.

"I've got something really important that I need to do, and it's pretty far away from here. It will probably take me awhile, but what if I come back this way when I'm done and see how you're getting along? If it turns out that it doesn't work out for you at all, and you still want to go, I'll go with you to help find this Deven friend of yours in the city, and we'll see about you living with them. Maybe even get one of those famous 'cheeseburgs' on the way. How would that be?

"In the meantime, though, what is it you promise to do for me?"

Jack looked at Elijah and smiled. "Whatever it takes," he proudly nodded, basking in the joy of knowing that Elijah cared enough about him to come back. He had no idea where his new best friend came from, or where he was going, but those things weren't really important. What he did know was that he liked baseball cards, and that he knew about being alone, and that he was coming back, just to check on him.

Elijah put the cards back in the box and told Jack that it was probably time to get going.

"What time do you have to do the sweeping at the store today?"

"Usually first thing in the morning on Saturday, but I can get there anytime really. Mrs. Wheaton doesn't mind," Jack replied.

"Well, I'll walk you back that way. Maybe I can get another big drink out of that faucet before I head back down the road."

"Sure," Jack offered. "I can get you another soda to take with you if you want."

On the walk back to the store, there was time for Jack to ask all the questions on his mind; where he came from, why he didn't have a car, had he actually slept outside, on the ground, what he did when it rained?

"If you get the chance to travel around a bit," Elijah told him "you really should. That is, of course, when you are old enough to take care of yourself on the road. There is no better way to see things and get to know interesting people. How else would we have met, my young friend?"

At the store, Jack ran inside to get a refreshment advance on his daily wage. When he returned outside, Elijah was at the faucet soaking a handkerchief in the cold well water. Tying it loosely around his neck, with a long "aaahhhhh" as he did it, he explained how that would help him stay cool as he walked the road in the hot sun.

"The good thing about these late season hot days, though, is they're shorter, right?" he asked Jack in jest. It was a comment intended to give Jack an on the spot lesson in looking at the brighter side of things.

Not yet fully grasping the science involved in shorter days versus cooler weather, or rhetorical questions for that matter, Jack nodded with an 'if you say so' kind of acknowledgment, and followed with the inevitable; "When do you think you'll be back?"

"I can't say exactly, Jack. But I sure don't want you looking down this road for me everyday. My best guess would be about a month, six weeks maybe," answered Elijah, as he slung the guitar over his shoulder.

"Okay, I guess I'll see ya then, Mister Elijah!" said the stone-faced boy.

"Yes, you will, Mister Jack!" smiled Elijah as he stared out at the road as if to prep himself mentally for the journey.

Turning to leave, Elijah stopped, turned back again, and walked toward the porch where Jack had taken a seated position with his legs dangling off the side. The elevation of the porch and the fact that Jack was sitting made for the two to be eye to eye as Elijah stood in front of him and stretched out his hand for Jack to grasp. Years later, Jack would always think back to that handshake. There was something about the way Elijah looked at him as they stood there shaking hands without speaking. In that brief human connection, Jack was provided with some small amount of relief, not unlike that felt by someone lost at sea when first glimpsing the shore lights. It is the relief which hope provides.

Before Elijah had turned around and walked back toward the porch, Jack felt sad enough that he wasn't sure he wouldn't break down and cry. He didn't really have a best friend anymore, and he was sure Elijah would be if he stayed. But, he wasn't, and Jack was beginning to feel the emptiness of another loss in his life.

He hoped that Elijah would already be down the road if it turned out that he was unable to control himself. But, when he came back and took up his hand, and looked in his eyes, the knot in his stomach gave way to a very different feeling. Jack thought at first that it was a sense of assurance about his return that he felt. But, later he was sure that what he saw in Elijah at that moment was a picture of exactly how he himself wanted to be; someone who would care about a kid that he didn't even know, and someone brave enough to sleep outside alone.

Having had parents and lost them. Having been wrapped in the warm blanket of protection that parents unknowingly provide, and having had that blanket pulled away, Jack lived in perpetual fear. The comfortable peace of mind that belongs to a child who understands he is the paramount concern of an adult is, indeed, a feeling of security most often taken for granted. But, to miss it is to live in the cold.

Maybe it was because Elijah was older, or because he seemed to have already been through what Jack was facing. Whatever it was, Jack could see that there was absolutely no such fear in his eyes. And to not be afraid anymore was all Jack wanted to be.

"Thanks for everything my friend!" Elijah said as he walked away.

"Don't forget where I am," Jack said as he waved with a smile. He rested his head on the porch rail and watched long enough to see him disappear into the depression down the road, then he turned and walked up the stairs to the store, took up the broom, and began to slowly sweep the porch.

Jack found it difficult to fall asleep that evening. At first he was trying to imagine where Elijah would be sleeping, then thinking about the next day being Sunday, and trying to figure out what he could offer to do before Mr. Gilchrest asked him.

Captain Keogh's horse, Comanche, was the sole survivor of General Custer's five companies at the Battle of the Little Big Horn.

He was being sold at an Army surplus auction years later, and as the prospective buyer

checked the soundness of his teeth, he looked into the horse's eyes and asked

"How is it that you survived that massacre 'ol boy?"

"Lucky!" said the horse. "Friends not so."

Convinced he couldn't have heard what he heard, the man spoke again,

"Must have been a lot of Indians."

"Not sure..... but an abundance of arrows," the horse grinned.

"Interesting that a horse can speak," noted the man.

"Interesting that a man can listen," chided the horse.

Chapter Eight

History

Michael, while feeling out of place the entire time, managed to have a wonderful dinner at Jaycee's. She had prepared a duck, which he had only eaten in a restaurant a few times in his life, in a sauce that he raved about several times during the evening.

After the meal, Jaycee introduced Michael to the perfect dessert for a such an elegant dinner. She had been saving a 1963 Taylor Fladgate Port wine for a special occasion, and decided this was as good a time to share it as any. Michael admitted to never having tried one, at least none he could recollect. With the first sip from the glass Jaycee handed him, after she had spent the longest time carefully decanting the bottle, he was quite sure he had never had anything like it before.

"Oh, my!" was his reaction to the first sip. "I always thought Port would be so sweet. I think that's why I never had the urge to try it. But, this is...., well, this is absolutely wonderful."

"I'm really glad you like it. This happens to be a classic year, so I have to warn you, you're liable to be slightly disappointed when you compare your next one to this.

"Enjoying fine wine was one of the few things I had in common with my former husband." she reflected after a slow sip from the tiny glass.

"My wife and I were champagne lovers. We would scrimp to buy Dom Perignon for very special occasions." Michael said with the kind of distant gaze such a memory brings.

"From everything I hear, it sure sounds like the two of you were truly happy," Jaycee commented.

"No doubt she was definitely 'the one', though I sometimes wish that she wasn't. Perhaps if I didn't feel that way, I don't know, maybe it would have made it easier to start a new life with someone else after. Since my wife passed away, I have occasionally felt that maybe the best thing might be to settle for someone who I did not feel as strongly about. Maybe I should be looking more for a mother for Kate than another perfect mate for me. But, I just couldn't. I mean I can't. It just wouldn't be fair," he professed while shaking his head.

While neither of them was exactly certain about the intent of the message, or even if there was any intent, the pained look he portrayed as he said it put asunder any consideration that Jaycee had given to the possibility of a relationship between her and he progressing. Not that she was even convinced that such a relationship was something to consider. But, it had become pretty clear to her at that moment that he had probably already found, and unfortunately lost, the only woman he would ever love.

The mild sadness that came upon her was more due to the vastly different directions from which they had come to this standoff. Jaycee, having been married to the wrong person from the start, was somewhat skeptical about there even being such a thing as a perfect mate, and if there was, she was quite sure she would go through life without ever finding him. Michael, she realized, represented living proof that such a thing was possible. He had actually experienced it, and as devastating an experience as it must have been to have lost it, he did, at least, enjoy the experience. The thought of love lost made her think of her son, and it was difficult to be more than melancholy from that point.

Sensing he had trampled the moment, Michael apologized for being such a "wet blanket". He told her that the reason he didn't date was because he knew he would somehow end up talking about his wife. He attempted to change the direction of the mood with a light comment about having been given several dating tips over the years and none of them mentioning the praising of one's prior spouse.

Jaycee assured him that it was fine, and that she knew they both had very serious scars from losing loved ones, so she understood the unshakable grief that accompanies that kind of loss. She explained that she was very happy for the fact that he seemed to have the chance to experience such rare passion in his life, and she felt confident that he had, at least, found a way to be happy with having Kate to fill some of the void.

At the end of the evening, Michael held her in his arms as she put her head on his shoulder. He stroked her hair and told her that she had become very special to him, and that he truly hoped she would find happiness again.

The kiss goodnight lasted more than a few seconds. It was the first real kiss either had experienced in several years and, while awkward in the coming together, was surprisingly warm and comfortable from the outset. Though both felt the trace of a spark within an instant, each resisted the urge to explore the emotion and, instead, made the conscious effort to finish with all the proper mechanics given a delicate kiss among friends. The slight dizziness they experienced in the aftermath was conveniently, silently, attributed to the wine.

Jaycee smiled as Michael thanked her for a fabulous evening and turned to leave.

"Thank you," she replied, intending the gratitude for his honesty.

In the weeks since Kate saw Elijah last, she had completed her make up course in science and brought the grade up to a 'B+'. Between all the tutoring sessions and the riding lessons, Kate and Jaycee had spent a considerable amount of time with one another since the meeting at 'The Big Sky' during the summer, and both sensed that a very special bond was developing between them.

Kate reminded Jaycee a lot of herself when she was that age, and she very much enjoyed helping her cope with that awkward age by sharing her experience and doing all she could to help boost her confidence.

In Kate's eyes, Jaycee had become something of a very caring older sister, one with whom she felt comfortable talking to about anything, and in whose judgment she had a high degree of confidence.

During one of the riding lessons on a Sunday afternoon, Kate took Jaycee up to the meadow. While there, the conversation turned to what Kate thought about doing after high school, and Jaycee made a comment about how she couldn't believe it had been so many years since her own high school graduation.

"God," she reflected, "this makes almost eighteen years since I was leaving Classical High. That's just hard to believe."

"Classical High? In Massachusetts?" Kate asked in surprise.

"Yes," Jaycee turned. "Had I mentioned that before?"

"Not that I remember." answered Kate. "I met someone else that went there, though."

"Went to Classical? Get out of here!" said the wide-eyed Jaycee in disbelief.

Kate told her the whole story about how she came to meet Elijah in this very place, and how she came back to meet him again a second time. Jaycee's facial expression before the story was even finished let Kate know that there would probably be the same lack of understanding about this stranger that Mallory exhibited. Actually, it was worse.

Jaycee seemed horrified at the prospect of some drifter luring a young girl into the wilderness alone. She asked Kate, calmly, if she had lost her mind. Having been raised in an urban environment back east, such open trust was always interpreted as naive recklessness.

"First of all, Kate, you said he looked like he was not much older than yourself," continued Jaycee. "Well, he happened to pick a school which closed the year after I graduated, so, unless you think he might be a very well preserved thirty four year old, he was obviously lying. Now, if he is lying to you about where he comes from, and whether or not he even *went* to high school, do you really believe he deserves your trust?"

Realizing that she was quickly outflanked in this battle, and reeling a bit at the same time from the sting of the news about the possible lie, Kate hastened a retreat.

"I know now that it was foolish. Believe me, I don't expect you to understand why this boy seemed to me to be so sincere. Maybe I was wrong about the high school. I may have just gotten the name wrong. Anyway, I'm not arguing that what I did was smart, but it's pretty obvious that he meant me no harm.

"Since it's over, and nothing bad happened, I don't see why my dad would need to be bothered with this, do you?" Kate asked rather timidly.

"I have no reason to bring it up, Kate. I don't think I would feel right, though, about lying to your father if he asked me directly about it. But, I guess if you're not going to tell him that probably won't happen.

"I do hope you understand, Kate, I worry about you. If it seems like I'm overreacting, it's only because I think about what could happen, and *does* happen, to women that are so trusting sometimes. I would hate for you to live in fear of people but, at the same time, you *have* to exercise *some* amount of caution when dealing with someone you don't know."

Amidst the small talk on the ride back from the meadow, Kate thought about what Jaycee had said, and felt comforted about how much she obviously meant to her. She also tried to recall the details of the conversation she had with Elijah, particularly the part when he mentioned which high school he had attended. She was very sure he had told her it was in Massachusetts, and she was *pretty* sure he had said Classical. "Probably not the only Classical High in Massachusetts," she thought.

Unfortunately, since she had pretty much made up her mind that he would not be coming back, she began to regret the idea of not knowing whether or not he did actually lie to her, and, if he did, why? She could only come up with two possible reasons for not being truthful about something like that. Either he dropped out of high school and was embarrassed to admit it, which she quickly ruled out because he seemed much too smart. Or, he really was in some trouble and was just trying to avoid telling her anything that could be used to find him. Of course, that would mean he didn't really trust her at all, so that couldn't be right either. She finally consoled herself with the idea that it was probably another school.

When Kate mentioned that Elijah had told her he would come back to meet her in about two more weeks,

Jaycee made her promise, on her honor, not to go out alone to meet him. As it happened, Kate realized a week before the prearranged rendezvous that it was going to land on the same day she was to take the S.A.T. exam. Certain that there was no way she would be able to get home in time to ride up to the meadow and back before dark, she decided to go up the weekend before and tack a note, sealed in a plastic sandwich bag, to the log on which they sat together.

"Dear Elijah:" it read, "I don't really expect you will be reading this, but, just in case, I wanted you to know that I didn't forget your promise, but I have to take my college entrance exams today, so I can't make our rendezvous.

"I hate the fact that I may never know if you did actually come by and just not find this note. But, I have come to think that you were never really intending to come back. If, by chance, I am wrong, please call me tonight (I'm the only Bennet in the book). I would really love to hear from you. Or, you can come back here tomorrow at noon. I'll bring the snacks, just in case. Kate."

During the grueling, four hour, brain busting ordeal commonly referred to as 'S.A.T.' day, Kate knew that each of the more than occasional distractions given to thinking about whether he might be at the meadow waiting for her was costing her valuable points. While she had no misconception about being pursued by the Ivy league, like every kid on this day she knew that the test results would be known by everyone, and the desperation to just come out so as not to look stupid created about all the stress she could handle. When the time had expired for the last exam, she walked out of the room with her head still spinning.

"Kate! How'd you do?" chimed an all too perky Mallory on the stairs leading down to the parking lot.

"I think I may have gotten a couple of those questions right," Kate answered looking dazed.

"Super!" responded Mal. "A couple of questions right, and the correct spelling of your name, and you nailed at least a 380. That should be all you need for most of the big colleges," she chided.

"Well, at least it is over," Mal noted. "Now we just sweat it out for five or six weeks until the bad news arrives."

Mallory was one that did okay in school, not great, but she put almost no effort into it. Kate had seen desperate spurts over the years, when last minute assignments were due, or when surprise quizzes came about, which caused her to believe Mallory was actually much more intelligent than she pretended to be. She was sure Mal would end up scoring much higher than her on the S.A.T. tests, with less than half of the stress.

Later that evening, having soaked away the tension of the day in a forty-minute hot shower, Kate sat on her porch in pajamas, robe and slippers, enjoying the peaceful darkness of the new moon. Her father had gone to an auction in Denver for the night, and wouldn't be home until sometime the following day. Normally when her dad was out of town, Kate would stay at Mal's or have her come over for the evening. After the stress of test day, though, Kate didn't feel like going along with the plan to go to "The Rack" for the evening. So, despite the onslaught of Mallory's begging, she told her she just didn't feel up to going and that she would be fine at home by herself for the night.

"What do I tell Keith? I promised him you would be there tonight," pleaded Mallory earlier that afternoon.

"Well, there you go Mal. If you are going to keep my social calendar for me, you're just going to have to get better at covering for me when I don't make it," Kate informed her.

Sipping hot tea and relaxing on the porch in front of the telescope was exactly what she felt like doing, and as she sat there that evening, doing just that, she was very content in having made the right choice.

At the very moment that all of her concentration was given up to her surprise at how many stars she could see in the Plaedies cluster *other* than the famous 'seven sisters', a voice rang out from the darkness, piercing the peaceful stillness, and sending all of her systems into a frenzy.

Somewhere between the leap out of the chair and the teacup hitting the floor there was a moment when she thought she recognized the voice, but, her mind was incapable of matching voice patterns while in the panic mode. It wasn't until she looked over toward the porch stairs, with eyes opened to their very light gathering limit, and could make out that it was Elijah standing there in the darkness, that her breathing began again.

"God, I can't believe you. Are you just trying to kill me?"

"I didn't think anyone was home," he assured her. "I couldn't see you there in the dark until I was right next to the porch. I thought I would just leave a note on your door. I am so sorry I frightened you, *again*." She sat back down gripping her chest as though it could ease the pounding going on inside. She looked over and realized her semi-retired watchdog was lying on his side with his head propped up staring back at her, as if he wondered what all the fuss was about.

"That's it!" she announced. "It's definitely time for a new watch dog. I could have been killed and he probably never would have gotten up."

Kate stood up as she caught her breath, turned on the small lamp on the table next to her, and walked toward the stairs.

"Nice shoes!" he said, as he walked up the few stairs onto the porch. The lamp shed just enough light to make the Goofy heads on her slippers appear even larger than they were.

"They're slippers!" she corrected him, now at arm's length. "They are a gift from my dad, and they are very comfortable, so we don't joke about these around here."

"Well, there was no joke intended. I like them, and I am honestly sorry I scared you, really! I was as surprised to see you sitting there as you were me. You were so focused on what you were looking at you must not have heard me walking up the driveway."

"All I know," she said half smiling as she moved closer and gave him a hug, "is that I owe you a *couple* of good scares now, my friend. And that's a debt I *will* be looking to repay one of these days."

"It's great to see you again too," he hugged her back.

"You got my note then?" she asked, as she took his arm and lead him to a chair.

He confirmed that he had just come from the meadow, where he read her note, but he wanted to find her so he could let her know that he couldn't meet her the next day.

"Well, how *did* you find me?" she asked.

"Very pleasant, actually," he mused while attempting a Groucho Marx impression. "That's why I came all the way back to see you."

The telltale squint of her confusion at both the spontaneity of the comment, as well as the rather cute impression, immediately gave way to a furled eyebrow, head nodding kind of chuckle when his answer registered.

"Actually, your address is 'in the book' as well," he said before she could critique his humor.

"Well, I'm glad you came," she confirmed, still smiling. "I'm dying to hear about your travel, but let me get you something to drink first. Coke, Dr. Pepper, Tea?" she offered as she began picking up the pieces of the broken teacup.

"If there isn't any Nugrape, a cold Coke would be great," he answered.

"No grape of any kind, old or new I'm afraid." she acknowledged as she disappeared across the porch and through the kitchen door. "But, Coke we have."

"Anything in particular you're searching for out here?" Elijah called out from the porch.

"I was about to look for Aldebaran," she spoke out so he could hear her. I think it's my favorite. Something mysterious about it, 'eye of the bull' and all. But, before you scared me, *again*," she emphasized, "I was focused on the Plaedies."

"The seven sisters could occupy your whole night, but I have to admit I'm inclined to agree that there is something mysterious about Aldebaran," he added.

Elijah noticed a large sheet of paper lying on the table beside him as he spoke, and sat forward to look at it more closely. It first appeared to be a dark colored sketch with some paint applied, but as he studied it in the dim light, he was able to make out that it was done in different shades of pencil on glossy yellow paper. It was a night scene of a cabin by a lake, and the yellow was left uncovered only to make the window of the cabin appear lit, a crescent moon, and slivers of light reflecting off the water. In the lower corner, written in what appeared to be a kind of gold lettering, was the word Utah.

"This is really beautiful," He told her, holding it out as she returned with his bottle of Coke.

"Sort of tried to capture the memory of my grandparent's place. We seemed to go there quite often when I was young. It was a beautiful old cabin on the water."

"What about a snack?" she asked. "I was going to pack these with some lunch tomorrow, hoping you would be there," she said holding out a pack of Twinkies.

"Thanks, Kate. Really, thanks for thinking of that," Elijah said as he took the drink and the package from her. "And, I'm sorry if I embarrassed you. I shouldn't have examined it without permission. I know how personal that stuff is. I spent a lot of my time in high school trying to put my feelings more into words than art, but it was very personal to me. Unfortunately, I'm sure I wasn't as talented as you seem to be, at least based on this drawing."

Thanking him, and feeling even closer now with his confession about having also been something of a writer, she told him how, contrary to his compliment, inept she felt with words.

"I mean, for instance, look out at that view!" she exclaimed, pointing to the stars. "To have the slightest understanding of what we are in the 'grand scheme'," she paused, "most of the time I think words, especially mine, can't possibly convey any of that."

"I know exactly what you mean," Elijah concurred as he looked out at the sky, "but you know, Kate, it seems to me that whether it's color, or notes of music, or words, some artist always comes along that somehow finds a way to stir people's emotions with their particular interpretation of them. And I think we need that.

"You could be the one."

Kate began to stumble through a comment to sound humble, lost her train of thought, and quickly recovered changing the subject; "So, do *you* have a favorite?" she inquired, reverting back to his question about her favorite star.

"I guess I'm probably partial to Sirius," he confessed after pausing for a moment to follow the segue.

"The Dog Star?" You too?" she seemed surprised.

"Well, it *is*, after all, the brightest, so I'm guessing that would be a pretty popular favorite," Elijah added. His tone made the choice seem obvious. "But, that's not really why it happens to be my favorite." he went on. "I think it's because it was the first thing in the sky that was ever really explained to me with passion.

"There is this popular analogy of Sirius being something of an opera, though I don't remember the details. I wasn't exactly familiar with the passion of opera at the time I heard it, but it made this tiny light seem like something much more complex than I had imagined. The comparison meant much more to me once I finally experienced the passion in the music when 'Alfredo' lost his 'Violetta' in Verdi's 'La Traviata'. My first, and only, opera", he sighed.

"That's really odd." Kate confided. "I have a teacher that seems to have that same kind of passion for the stars. She even remembered the same analogy about the Dog Star and its twin.

"She gave us this telescope, as a matter of fact."

"Probably watched 'Cosmos' like most of us, but it does sound like the kind of teacher worth listening to," he suggested.

"Yeah, I think so," she agreed.

It was quiet for a moment as she reflected on how good Jaycee had been to her, and she immediately felt a twinge of guilt about the promise made to bring her along when seeing Elijah again.

Changing the subject again, Kate began to tell him how difficult it was to take the S.A.T. while being distracted by the thought of whether or not he might be waiting for her, when he suddenly interrupted her.

"Whether or not?" he interjected.

"I guess I kind of made up my mind that you only said you were coming back to make it easier to leave," she admitted sheepishly.

"Sagittarius really is a cynical sign isn't it?" he asked, nodding and looking down as though feigning disappointment.

Delaying her answer for a few seconds as her mind sorted through the only other two conversations they had, to remember if she had somehow unwittingly told him her birth date, and, feeling fairly sure she hadn't, decided to call his bluff.

"As a matter of fact, I'm a Scorpio," she corrected him with a straight face.

"Scorpio? No kidding?" he questioned in mock surprise. "That's too bad. I thought you shared a sign with the likes of Winston Churchill, Beethoven, and Mark Twain, not to mention, of course, Dick Clark and Jesus."

"Okay, I was just trying to throw you off. I was born on the 5th of December."

"Really? That's the same birthday as Disney, and Custer," he announced. "Though I can't imagine why that would be significant. I can't think of much in common with those two, although now that I think about it they *are* famous enough to be known by just one name," he smiled.

"When you think about it, these were two guys that had distinctly different ideas about how to create a tourist attraction, wouldn't you say?

"Okay, I'm sorry, I guess I'm rambling again."

"Why would you know that? I mean, how do you know who was born on that day?" a bewildered Kate asked.

"I don't know. That's just some of the trivia that you read somewhere and end up storing in the 'interesting facts' file," he explained.

Kate started to ask if the rest of the people he mentioned were really Sagittarius, or if he was just making it up, when she realized that he said "Jesus".

"Wait, wait, wait, just hold on. Did you say Jesus?" she questioned. "That's late December there, Mr. History! So that would be a, uh…"

"Mister History?" he chided.

"Capricorn?" he added as though she had to be kidding. "Jesus?

"Somewhere I read that the 25th of December was kind of *arranged* by the Romans because there was a bit of a gap in the holiday schedule around that time, January was already a pretty full month. Let's face it, if they moved it back one more week, what have we got then?"

"Another *guess?*" she quipped. "Did you go to a Catholic school or something?"

Just as Kate said it she remembered where he did say he went to high school, which brought back the conversation with Jaycee. Her expression changed to all business almost instantly as she contemplated how to politely challenge the Classical High 'story', and the transition was noticeable.

Elijah, sensing the change, kept silent, holding his chin between his thumb and forefinger and staring into space. His eyes seemed to drift slowly from the stars to the telescope, pausing there to think for a few moments, and then to Kate, looking almost through her at first, and then coming to focus on her returned stare.

"Mr. Galilei," he posed, his voice now sounding tired. "Do you suppose he sometimes wonders if we might look past what we need to see?"

Kate found herself pulling back the question about being lied to, and quickly retracing all the steps in the conversation in order to try to figure out exactly why she had no idea what he was talking about. Her attempt to rethink the timing of the interrupted accusation, combined with the desperate search for where exactly she might have missed the clue that might help her to understand the meaning of his question, resulted in a bit of an overload. At the same time, and almost as concerning, was the noticeable change in his tone. Kate suspected that the subtle change in his voice was not the result of a long day on the road. She was suddenly struck with the strange feeling that he had already understood her concern about some of what he had told her, and that it might be a bit of disappointment she was detecting.

"Mr. Galilei?" was the result of all that she could think to answer, hoping that he would see she had given up the idea of pressing him for more answers.

"Yes. Mr. *Galileo* Galilei," he answered, pointing at the telescope while making it seem that no answer was exactly what he was hoping for.

"You know! The one credited with first aiming this contraption at the sky."

Turning toward her, he apologized for the digression, his enthusiasm seemed renewed as he turned back to peer through the scope.

"But, you know, I spent some time reading about Galileo, and the more I learned about him the more I thought of him as something of a hero. Not only because he was a genius, but he dared to stand by what he believed, even when everyone he knew thought he was either a fool or a heretic.

"The reason I think that all this might make for an interesting study for *you* is that Galileo was, well, it strikes me that he was kind of like you in some ways, I think. I mean, he constantly wondered about things. I don't think he was comfortable taking anything for granted. "

Kate mentioned that she remembered covering Galileo in one of her classes, and how he was persecuted in some sort of court for writing that the earth revolved around the sun. She admitted that it didn't peak her interest when she first learned of it because such foolish things that happened in the "dark ages" didn't seem all that relevant.

"Yeah, I know what you mean. I was the same way with history. But, let me ask you this," Elijah proposed after thinking for a while. "Since you took your college entrance test today this fact should be fresh in your mind. Name the first English settlement in America."

"Jamestown, Virginia, of course," she replied confidently.

"Of course," he concurred. "And *after* Jamestown was settled, and the first English babies born in the new settlement grew up and had children of their own, *that's* about when Galileo was facing the inquisition in Italy for writing that the earth was not the center of the universe."

"That's true?" Kate asked in disbelief. She suddenly realized that all she learned having to do with the discovery and settlement of the "New World" had somehow been filed in her mind under modern history, and everything to do with Europe was under ancient history. The idea that the relationship of the earth to the sun was not settled as recently as people were coming to America made her feel as though she missed some important step in understanding exactly what she had been taught in the eleven long years of schooling, and that her snippets of historic events had been segmented into separate and unrelated events.

"I'm embarrassed," she admitted while shaking her head. "I guess I never thought to put together what things were going on when. The idea of getting to America seemed so advanced, and the thought of persecuting someone for believing in a particular way seemed so ancient. But, thinking about it now, we did have the witch trials here in America not long after that, didn't we?"

"Right!" he asserted. "And the Scopes trial only a few centuries later. But, getting back to Galileo, I've got another one of those time association questions for you, if you will indulge me. Who came first, Shakespeare or Galileo?"

Kate knew that she wasn't really sure, but since the point seemed to be that Galileo was around more recently than she would expect, she decided to opt for the least obvious option.

"Shakespeare?" she guessed with a voice of authority.

"That was a bit of a trick question, but no. It was Galileo by two months."

"Two months apart? Is that true?" asked the surprised Kate.

"You keep asking me that like I'm making this stuff up." Elijah smiled mischievously. "Just because I didn't get to college doesn't mean I can't read."

Kate apologized, delicately, and assured him that she believed what he was telling her. She commented on having a record for choosing wrong when given 50/50 choices, and that the idea of two men of such genius being born so close together seemed so far fetched."

Elijah agreed that it was quite an interesting coincidence, "Assuming," he added, "it was really William Shakespeare that wrote all those things."

Kate looked puzzled by the comment, and before she could ask about it he went on to say;

"But, that's a discussion for another time. Let's, for now at least, say that the real Mr. Shakespeare was arguably the greatest writer of all time."

Kate thought for a moment that this was the kind of exchange that she imagined might happen in college. Professors totally engrossed in their subjects posing interesting questions that would make the student piece together ideas and want to know more.

"So, what else did you learn in your study of Galileo?" Kate asked with renewed interest.

"I almost forgot why I brought him up in the first place," Elijah said after stopping to think for a moment. "I thought of him the last time we talked about that whole circle of knowledge idea. The things that are dreamed, or discovered, that we didn't even know we didn't know about, it sometimes contradicts what we always *believed* to be true. That tends to create problems. The greater the belief, the more resistance.

"Think about this," Elijah sat forward to emphasize. "Galileo, at the ripe old age of *nineteen* mind you, before the time of clocks, looked at a lamp swinging inside of a cathedral and figured out that the distance of the arc was always equal from the center. As simple as that sounds, it was the foundation of utilizing a pendulum for keeping time. More than fifty years later, after he had become blind, Galileo went back to work on this idea and worked out the pendulum theory that Huygens used to put together the first clock.

"When he was forty-five he heard of someone in Holland aligning lenses in a way that magnified things. Deciding to do his own experimenting with lenses he came up with a telescope to study the sky. That makes him a bit of a master with both time *and* space, don't you think?" he joked, checking to see if Kate was still listening.

Seeing her smile in appreciation of the humor, and delighted he hadn't put her to sleep, he continued. "Maybe the real irony in his life was that while he was teaching the Ptolemy basis for the earth centered universe at the University of Padua in Italy, he was beginning to realize that Copernicus was actually right. By noting the movement of Jupiter and Venus, he became certain that the earth couldn't possibly be standing still. And so the conflict began, with what was believed versus what could be proven, and, as we know, the believers won that battle.

"Anyway," he went on after a long pause, "I can't imagine Galileo ever thought that he would be remembered for putting together a telescope. He had, after all, much 'bigger fish to fry' with changing the entire understanding of the universe at that time. Can't you just imagine his excitement when he was finally convinced that he had the proof?" he asked with his voice raised. "And then his utter disappointment when he realized that no one wanted to believe him?

"Unfortunately, his eyes must have still been fixed on the stars when he underestimated how his learned colleagues would take his news, even with what he thought to be indisputable proof. The scholars of the time turned out to have blind faith in what was already 'known', and refused to buy into his lie."

Standing and walking in front of Kate to look into the telescope, Elijah continued; "Here was this new tool which he fashioned for a closer look at the heavens, to get a better understanding of the universe, and people looked through it with their eyes closed. What Galileo was telling them didn't fit with what they already knew, so," he paused as he walked back to the chair, "he *had* to be wrong."

Standing by the chair Elijah stopped again to think, and then went on to say that one of the things he remembered best from all that he had read about Galileo came from his "Letter to the Grand Duchess Christine of Lorraine", which he penned to defend his position when he was first attacked for his 'radical' discovery.

"In this letter," Elijah recounted, "he quoted one of the Cardinals at the time as saying the '*Holy Spirit intended to teach us in the Bible how to go to Heaven, not how the heavens go.*' I think the choice of such a profound statement to quote, and the fact that it was a quote from one of their own, made it an ingenious argument, maybe not a winning argument, but ingenious just the same."

When Elijah finished speaking, he took the bottle of Coke from the table, eased himself back in the chair, and slowly took a long drink, looking as though he was contemplating what to say next. Kate waited for him to continue, but he put the bottle back on the table and folded his hands in front of him, saying nothing more.

Using the silent pause to think, Kate was convinced that this story was not told by coincidence.

"You know, Elijah," Kate said staring out into the night. "I've never talked to anyone quite like you before.

You seem like this wise old man in a boy's body, and I don't know if it's just that you're so worldly, or that being here all my life has made me stupid.

"I do think, though, that I understand the message in your story, and I want you to know that you don't really need to feel obligated to explain anything to me.

"If you knew me," she added, "you would know that I would never say this, but, for some reason I feel like I need to." Stopping a moment to think about what she wanted to say, she leaned forward and looked directly into his eyes. "If you didn't seem so much like the brother I never had, Elijah, I might think you were the man of my dreams. And, I honestly do trust you, contrary to all the advice of the learned people of *my* time," she finished with a smile.

For the next few hours they talked about school, Kate's future, her Dad, Daniel, Jaycee and Duchess, and Jack.

When asked how it turned out when he went to help the friend he had told her about, Elijah explained that he never really made it to where he needed to be, but that he was going back again, and that this "would probably take some time".

"You are obviously convinced, though, that this person needs *your* help?" Kate asked.

"Fact is, I'm not totally sure. I wish I was, but I do know that I need do everything I can, and I haven't done that yet."

Again she realized that there were limits to what she could understand, and that it just might be that Elijah was doing the only thing he knew to do to help a friend. She made up her mind that *whatever* he was doing for someone in that kind of need, was surely better than doing nothing. What he was attempting to do, she felt, was important stuff, and she was certain that even if it was not within her ability to understand, it was still beyond her right to question.

When it was clear that Kate was yawning more than she was talking, Elijah told her that he really should be going so that she could get some sleep.

When Kate asked him where he would go, and where he would sleep, he told her that he passed a pretty safe place on the way to her house, and planned to head back that way.

"Please stay here tonight," she insisted. "You can have the pull-out bed in the living room, or I'll give you a blanket, and you can make yourself comfortable right here on the porch sofa if you like. Please, promise me you won't wander out looking for a place to camp at this hour."

"No, I won't wander then," he assured her. "If you insist, and you're sure it won't be a problem, I'll be more than comfortable right here on the porch."

"I do insist!" she announced while going into the house to get a blanket.

As Kate handed him a pillow and blanket, she asked how he seemed to know so much without having gone to college.

"I've had time to think about these things. Besides," he smiled, "I think college is a good place for people to go and open their eyes, and their minds, to new stuff. But, it's definitely not the only place a person can learn."

A bit embarrassed that she made it sound so stupid that anyone without a college degree must be less intelligent, Kate awkwardly agreed and then said a quick "Goodnight and sleep well" as she turned to leave

"Thanks, again, for everything!" he said as she was walking back into the house.

The clock read 5:35 when Kate awoke suddenly. From her bed she could see the first inkling of light mixing with the darkness. Taken with the strangest feeling that there was something going on outside, while still groggy from having less than five hours sleep, she made her way to the window. In the stillness of the earliest transition from night to day, she could hear a stirring on the porch below her. She knelt there at the window and listened intently. Something was moving about very quietly, and Kate couldn't discern if it was the dog or Elijah.

Just when she couldn't hear it anymore, and was convinced that Elijah was still sleeping, she was startled to see him emerge from the cover of the porch roof and into view as he stepped quietly down the stairs leading from the porch.

"Leaving me?" she shouted, realizing immediately after she said it how loud it sounded.

"Jeez Louise," he whispered as he stumbled off the last stair. "Did you wait up all night for that pay back?"

"No, honestly, I didn't mean to scare you," she apologized in a laugh that was difficult to disguise. "I was just surprised to see you leaving."

"Well," he stalled for a moment, "I couldn't sleep much, and 'the early bird'...., you know."

"Would that be the crow or the raven this time?" she quipped.

He smiled and pointed at her with a congratulatory nod as he looked up toward the window.

"So, when will I see you again, Elijah?" she asked somberly.

"I don't know the answer to that," he admitted as the smile left his face, "but I will surely try to make it back here one day".

"I'm glad you're awake, though," he said still looking up. "I wanted you to know, about what you said last night. I want you to know that I would have been very proud to be either."

Still a bit groggy, but sure that he couldn't have been referring to the crow or the raven, she thought back to the conversation of the night before, and after a long pause asked "You mean Shakespeare or Galileo?"

"No. But I'll blame this one on the early hour. Actually I meant your brother or the man of your dreams," he smiled up at her as he turned to walk away.

"Don't forget. I'm not booked for the Prom, just in case you're back this way"

Turning back when he was halfway up the driveway he said in a loud whisper; "easily the best offer I've ever had, my lady friend, but then the boy with the one headlight would be so disappointed.

"But thanks, again, for your friendship and your trust in me, Kate. I definitely won't forget you."

She thought that she saw him wave goodbye as he turned and continued walking, but could barely see him at that point.

Resisting the temptation to run downstairs and chase him down the driveway for what she envisioned to be a long embrace, she instead shouted "please do come back" into the darkness.

As much as Kate's tendency was to generally look at things from a slightly more 'half empty' perspective, she was smiling as she knelt there. She was sure that Elijah was the most interesting and intelligent boy she had ever met, and was absolutely confident that this sort of chance encounter could not end so abruptly. As a picture of he and her at the prom crept into her mind, she recalled the "one headlight" comment, and assumed he was joking about her eventual date driving a 'clunker'.

Between the idea
And the reality
Between the notion
And the act
Falls the shadow

T.S. Eliot

Chapter Nine

Geography

For almost an hour Kate watched the dim light swell from the horizon, ever so slowly, changing dark, to gray, to light, in barely detectable degrees of magnitude.

It came to her that she had never thought to watch a sunrise start to finish. Still on her knees at the window, as if in the worship of nature, she became aware for the first time that daybreak was so much more than a simple glimpse of any colorful moment in the process. On this morning, it was as though she had been looking over a vast dark canvas, which was being painted tediously with subtle layers of slightly lighter shades, one by one, filling in far to near, until the landscape came to look exactly as she remembered it.

The sound of the phone ringing stirred her quickly from the semi-conscious state, and on the third ring the proper brain commands were initiated and muscle movements engaged which were necessary to react accordingly. The short distance between the window and nightstand where the phone was, however, took another three rings to traverse due to problems incurred with knees that had apparently assumed the contour of the hard surface upon which she had knelt so long.

"Don't tell me I woke you?" Kate's father countered to her "Hello?"

"Hey, Dad....No! No, I was just.... No, I've been up for awhile," she labored while sitting down on the bed and massaging her aching kneecaps.

Her father had called to check in and to make sure all went well on her night alone. Kate was tempted for a moment to tell him about her visitor, but quickly decided against it. She knew he would have considered it totally irresponsible, so after she assured him that she spent a rather restful evening staring into the sky through the telescope, he told her he would be home by mid afternoon and the conversation ended.

After sitting there for another few minutes, pondering the lie she told, she felt uneasy about the fact that it was now set, kind of like concrete, quickly drying into a permanent kind of problem. She didn't feel good about it when she realized that she couldn't just decide to change her story and tell him the truth if, or when, she changed her mind.

The phone rang again.

"It must be him calling back," she thought. "Maybe I should tell him now. Maybe it wouldn't look so bad if I confessed right away."

"Hello?" she said as she lifted the phone to her ear.

"Kate, did I wake you?" asked the voice.

Stunned for a moment having expected to hear her father's voice, Kate answered; "Jaycee?"

"Yes, I'm sorry. I guess I did wake you," Jaycee apologized.

"No, you didn't, really!" Kate assured her. "It is a popular question this morning, but no, you didn't. You just surprised me. I thought it was my dad calling."

"I didn't think you would be sleeping," admitted Jaycee. "I was wondering if you wanted to get an early ride in today. That is, if you're not busy."

"That would be great," Kate replied, thinking about how much she wanted to tell *somebody* about the night before. "Actually, I don't have anything going today."

Kate let Jaycee know that she needed to shower and get the morning chores done, so they settled on 9:30 for the ride.

Rushing through the shower process to get to the barn, Kate threw on some jeans and an Arizona State University T-shirt and ran down stairs. She poured a quick glass of juice to take with her and she was out the door on the way to the barn.

As she crossed the porch, she saw Elijah's guitar leaning against the wall by the table. It was in plain view, so she immediately got the feeling that he couldn't have forgotten it. Recalling his leaving only a few hours before, she did remember that he was not carrying the guitar on his shoulder as he walked away. But she didn't remember seeing it with him when he arrived either. She was sure that he must have had it and she just didn't notice.

The one thing that came to her when she realized that it was left there, most likely on purpose, was that it had to be an indication that he was sure to come back.

As she brought it up to her room to keep it out of sight from her father, she could see that there were letters carved inside the guitar, under the strings. Upon reaching the top of the stairs where there was more light, she was able to see that the letters were C.S.. This was concerning for a moment, for if they *were* initials they certainly weren't his, and if he lied about his name, what else might he have kept from her. But she decided it was more likely that he bought the guitar used, and the initials were just as likely those of the previous owner.

Putting it safely away in her closet, behind the large box, which she kept full of stuffed animals, she ran back down stairs and into the barn.

Jaycee arrived sporting a new western hat. Kate was walking the horses out of the barn when she caught sight of her getting out of her car. It was a traditional style black hat with a silver band, and her dark hair was in a braid behind her. Kate was thinking that since she had known Ms. Turner, her French teacher all through her junior year, she never remembered her hair being anything but straight. It was one of the things she first noticed about her, because it was the kind of hair that Kate would have given anything to have, the thick shiny kind of hair that seemed to fall into place no matter how her head turned. Seeing her standing there with a French braid and a cowboy hat, Kate had to smile as she thought about the impact a horse could have on a person.

Kate decided they would probably ride out toward the place Jaycee gave her the astronomy lesson since she hadn't ridden that way in a long time. It was a bit too windy to go up country to the meadow and, although the sky didn't look threatening, there was a cloudbank developing way off to the west that looked like it might produce some rain later in the day. Not wandering too far seemed like a good idea to her.

After dispelling Jaycee's concern about her dad being out of town, and whether she was frightened being alone, Kate suggested they head out. I wish you would have called me, Kate," Jaycee said as she mounted Duchess. "You know you could have stayed at my house."

Kate reminded Jaycee that she was almost seventeen, and explained that she felt quite old enough to be staying home alone without people worrying about her.

Jaycee apologized and admitted that she really did have confidence that Kate was more than capable of looking out for herself. She told her that the only reason she brought up the offer was to assure her that if she *did* ever need a place to stay in that situation, she would hope that she knew it was a standing invitation. Kate thanked her for that.

Walking the horses north kept them from facing the wind, and the dust being kicked up in its path. It wasn't something Kate gave thought to when choosing the destination, but it worked out well. It would have been a little more difficult conversing if they were trying to keep the dust out of their faces while heading into the wind.

About a half mile out, Jaycee was talking about being asked to serve on the committee for arranging an "interim" reunion for her high school graduating class the following year. She was telling Kate how excited she was about the idea since there hadn't been a 15th reunion because no one could be found that had the time to coordinate it at the time, and she was really looking forward to seeing everyone again.

This seemed to Kate to be the perfect timing for her confession.

"Speaking of high school, Jaycee," she began. "Do you remember the boy I told you I met who said he attended the same school?"

"Oh yes, I certainly do remember that story, Kate." Jaycee exclaimed. "You had me worried with that boy!"

"Well, the thing is, I saw him again last night." As Kate said it, Jaycee pulled Duchess up close enough so that she could cause both horses to stop.

"What?" Jaycee said staring directly into Kate's eyes. "You made me a promise!" she reminded her with a look of shock.

"He said he would be back yesterday, and he came back," Kate explained with a 'please don't be mad' sort of expression. "What was I supposed to do, tell him to go away? Tell him I don't trust him because he wasn't straight with me about his high school?" she went on.

"Yeah, that's what I guess I *hoped* would happen," Jaycee said, her face reflecting her utter disappointment.

"Well," Kate offered. "Once again, he obviously meant me no harm. He was at my house all night and, I assure you, he never even tried anything."

Jaycee was visibly shocked by the announcement. "All night?" was all she could come out with in her surprise.

"I convinced him to sleep on the porch rather than find someplace outdoors last minute, and he was the perfect gentleman," Kate boasted. "He was off again at first light."

"I don't know what to say," Jaycee said, still flustered. "I just can't believe it," she went on. "This guy, who you know *nothing* about, stayed at your house while you were alone. I just don't believe it, Kate. It doesn't seem like something you would do. It's just crazy!"

"I *know* that you can't understand. No one would. I sure don't understand it," Kate admitted. "There is something about this guy, Jaycee. There is no way for me to explain it to you, but I know him as well as I know myself. He is the most amazing person I have ever met."

"And what," Jaycee interjected, "did this most amazing person have to say about the little lie he told you?"

"We didn't discuss it, actually," she sheepishly replied. "Again, there is no way I can make you see the sense in this because you haven't met him. You can't know what he means to me. I've even considered going to find him, Jaycee. I feel like he's that important to me right now."

"You are scaring me," Jaycee told her, moving even closer. "You listen to me, sweetheart. I have come to care a great deal about you, and I can't sit by and watch you come apart over some 'pied piper' like drifter. This time you are going to promise me, and *mean* it. If this guy contacts you again, you and I are going to meet him. Now, you understand this time that it doesn't mean you go to meet him, and *then* you and I. It means you and I *together*. Will you promise me that, and keep this promise, Kate?"

"I promise!" she answered. "I really want you to meet him anyway. It's the only way you will understand what I am telling you."

"Well, this time I hope you keep it," Jaycee reiterated. "Now, all you have to do is figure out a way to tell your dad."

Kate had a feeling it would come to that. She knew she couldn't ask Jaycee to keep this secret. She hadn't planned to. She was pretty sure she was going to have to tell him anyway. It was only a matter of how, and when.

Turning back south to head home, it became immediately noticeable that the wind had picked up, and shifted slightly from west to southwest. Looking straight into the wind, Kate could see that the bank of clouds that looked so distant just an hour before was making much better progress towards them than she had anticipated.

The conversation on the ride back was minimal. They galloped on and off to try to make up time, but the rain came with almost a mile left to go. Kate kept a slicker in her saddlebag, and offered it to Jaycee just before it began. But, since Jaycee was in a sweatshirt, and Kate only had a T-shirt, it was quickly decided that she should wear it herself.

By the time they reached the barn, they were drenched. They had ridden the last mile with their shirts pulled up over much of their faces to avoid the sting of the pelting raindrops.

"Rode hard and put away wet. That's a cliché that never really meant anything to me until now," Jaycee stated as they tied the horses in the barn. After taking the saddles off as quickly as possible and putting a blanket on each of the horses, they ran to the house for some dry clothes and hot tea.

Kate's father came home about an hour after Jaycee left. As soon as he put his bag in his room and returned to the kitchen, Kate told him she needed to talk to him for a minute.

The confession didn't, as she fully expected, go over very well. Although he was grateful, he said, for her having enough respect to tell him the truth, he was *very* disappointed in her judgment. He made it quite clear that he expected that this would never happen again, but not because, he emphasized, he insisted upon it. He did his best to make Kate understand that his real hope was that she become mature enough to make responsible decisions on her own. That was the only way, he told her, that he could feel confident about her safety when she went off to college somewhere.

Two weeks passed since Kate last spoke with Elijah, and she was still thinking about him often. One Saturday morning, she and Jaycee had arranged to meet at the Big Sky for breakfast, to talk about college. Jaycee had agreed to help her review some possible choices and to assist her with the applications.

Kate spotted Jaycee in a booth near the door as she entered the diner. She slid into the seat directly across, exchanging smiles and morning greetings. Jaycee was writing on a pad of paper and seemed deep in thought when Kate arrived. She explained to Kate that she was finally answering the letter she received requesting that she join her high school reunion committee. In order to give Kate her full attention she put the pad of paper to one side and put the letter she had received on top of the pad.

Kate could see that on the letter was a copy of a photograph, and upside down from her view it still looked as though it could be a younger Jaycee.

"Is that an old picture of you?" Kate quizzed.

"Oh, yes." Jaycee admitted. "All the invitations will be sent with a copy of the yearbook photo on it. Not *my* idea, but this is how they sent me the request to help them out next year," she explained as she handed Kate the letter.

Kate stared at the photograph and didn't speak, her eyes wide as though she had seen a ghost.

"Jesus H!" Kate shrieked, uncharacteristically using one of her father's favorite expressions, and loud enough that Jaycee turned to see how many people suddenly looked over.

"Excuse me?" she asked.

"Your name," she paused. "It says Josephine?"

"Oh, that," Jaycee smiled. "I guess not many people around here would know about that. My best friend started calling me Jaycee, for my initials - Josephine Carol you know - in the 9th grade, and it stuck. I was just happy at the time to be called anything but Josephine, or Jo. Of course, they had to put the 'real' name in the yearbook."

"Can I look at your yearbook?" Kate requested, still looking a bit pale.

"Well, what is it, Kate?" asked Jaycee. "Why do you look like you've seen a ghost? And why do you need to see my yearbook, anyway?"

"Please, Jaycee it's important," Kate insisted. "Can we go to your house and look at the yearbook?"

"You mean now?" Jaycee asked in disbelief.

Kate looked very serious when she pleaded "Honestly, Jaycee, if it wasn't important I wouldn't ask."

On the way to her house, Jaycee pressed to know what the mystery was surrounding the yearbook, but Kate wasn't sure how to tell her. The subject of Elijah was not a popular one with Jaycee or her dad, so she figured it would be better if she found what she was looking for, whatever that was, in the yearbook. She was able to fend off the questions by saying that she would explain once she had seen it.

"I was *really* looking forward to having breakfast this morning, young lady," Jaycee jokingly complained as they entered the house. "So this had better be worth it."

Escorting Kate into the living room, she handed her the yearbook, which was still on the coffee table since pulling it out of the closet the day she received the letter. Kate sat quietly and reviewed each page. When she reached the end of the student pictures, having half expected to find Elijah, she felt a little embarrassed.

Suddenly she wasn't exactly sure what she had hoped to find.

"Well?" Jaycee inquired when she saw Kate come to the end of the book.

Turning back to a page she kept marked with her finger, Kate turned the book around for Jaycee to see. "This boy you are with," she pointed, "if you tell me he was the captain of the basketball team I will have a conniption."

Jaycee took the book in her hands, noticing that the picture taken of her and her boyfriend at the time was in a collage of photos appropriately titled "Couples." No names or captions accompanied the photos.

"Did you see him in the sports part of the book?" Jaycee asked curiously.

"He was, wasn't he?" Kate confirmed.

"Okay, Kate, you're scaring me. Can you please tell me what this is about?"

It was a long story, but Kate told her about her conversations with Elijah. She told her about how he liked someone in high school whose name was Josephine, but that she paid no attention to him because she was devoted to the basketball captain. She went on to tell her how sad he seemed that he missed his chance with this girl, and that he even played a song that he had written about her.

"This is *so* weird!" Kate exclaimed, putting her hands to her head. "It's like he could have been talking about you the whole time and I just didn't get it. He even *talked* about people being connected. I'm telling you, Jaycee, there's something strange about this. It just seems too weird to be coincidence."

"Let's not get crazy here. One thing is certain. If you are sure that he is close to your age, he didn't go to *this* high school," Jaycee stated holding out the yearbook. "This we know." Pausing for a few moments, she continued; "If this isn't a grand coincidence, then he must know someone who knew me back then I suppose. Or, he got hold of one of these yearbooks." Thinking for another moment, she went on again; "If he really is the age you say, he could I guess, I mean I suppose it is possible that he is the son of someone I knew back then.

"Do you have any idea what his last name is?"

Kate reluctantly admitted that he did not want her to know his last name.

"Why am I not surprised by that?" she sarcastically quipped.

"I thought it was because he might have been in some kind of trouble." Kate confessed.

Sensing that this news made Jaycee even more skeptical, Kate closed her eyes and concentrated as much as possible on the details of the conversation she had with Elijah. As she was trying to re-enact the dialog in her mind, it came to her.

"Navy blue sequins, white gloves and pearls," Kate said softly, pointing her finger as though she was answering a question.

"What?" Jaycee asked.

"Your prom outfit," she announced. " He said 'navy blue sequins, white gloves and pearls.'"

"Yes, well, that's in the book too." Jaycee hesitantly informed her. "I got elected to the Queen's Court, so our photos got in the 'Big Events' section." It was obvious in her face, however, that she was not totally convinced by her own reasoning.

"I'm telling you, Jaycee, this is too weird." Kate nodded as she thumbed to the section to have a look. "And it would be a stretch to say this dress is navy blue by looking at this black and white photo. Don't you think?" Kate argued as she pointed to the page.

"Okay, then he *has* to know someone that knew me back then." Jaycee reiterated.

"And he goes around singing the song someone *else* wrote for a high school flame." Kate jokingly concluded. "Yes, I think that would probably be the explanation."

"I'm sensing sarcasm there, Kate. Would you prefer that we call it a bizarre coincidence?" Jaycee countered.

"C'mon. Jaycee, something doesn't fit here. Even if I could buy the fact that he knows someone that knew *you* back then, he still must have known about *our* relationship. He had to know that I would tell you about this," Kate said slowly, gathering her thoughts as she spoke. "Maybe he really wanted to talk to you the whole time. Maybe he knew you wouldn't trust him. Who knows, Jaycee, he could be trying to get some information about someone *you* knew back then."

"I missed breakfast so I could have Charlie Chan over," Jaycee mused. "One thing is sure, Kate, you've got my curiosity peaked. Unfortunately, we don't have a clue who he is. And, I get the feeling you have no idea where he went from here. Am I right?"

"Pretty much!" she agreed. "All he said was that he was going back out to help a friend. He did say it was about 1300 miles away."

"Then I guess all we can hope for in order to solve this mystery is that he wanders back here someday," Jaycee said as she gathered the yearbook and put it back on the shelf. "Until that happens, I suppose it's out of our hands. For the moment, though," she said after pausing to look at her watch, "maybe we should head back over to the Big Sky and see what the lunch specials are?"

Kate remembered that she left a note at home for her dad telling him she would be home by noon, and it was 12:10. She called from Jaycee's and asked if he wanted to meet them at the Big Sky for lunch. After she kidded with him, saying that Jaycee made her call to see if she could get him to buy their lunch, he agreed.

"Having lunch with two beautiful women isn't an offer that comes around everyday," he told her. "So I suppose it would be well worth the expense."

On the way over to the restaurant, Jaycee told Kate that she planned to call her sister later that evening, because if there was anyone that knew anything about the people that attended Classical High, she did. Her sister, she explained, was a year behind her in high school. But, she was involved in everything according to Jaycee.

"If this kid's father went to my high school," Jaycee pondered, "and got married shortly after, I'd be willing to bet Denise would know something about it."

The subject was not discussed during lunch. Just as Jaycee pulled into the parking lot, she asked Kate if she talked to her father about the overnight visit. Upon learning that she had, she recommended waiting until they figured out who this guy was before she compounded her problem by telling her dad such a farfetched story.

After lunch they parted, Kate with her father, and Jaycee alone.

"I'll call you if I find anything out about that, Kate," were Jaycee's words as she pulled out of the parking lot.

"Finds out anything about what?" asked Kate's dad.

"Girl stuff, Dad." Kate quickly covered. "Nothing important," she assured him as she pulled the car slowly out into the road and headed toward home. Much to her surprise, he had offered to let her drive home as they approached the car in the parking lot.

On the phone with her sister that evening, Jaycee explained the events that she and Kate had discussed earlier that day. Jaycee realized after she had told her sister all the details she could remember from the conversation, that it sounded even more crazy than it had earlier.

"Well, Jo," her sister commented, "that's one hell of a story! For this boy to mention the school, the name, the dress? Sounds like it's a bit much to shrug off as a coincidence."

Denise admitted that she couldn't ever remember meeting anyone with the name Elijah, much less knew one from the old school. She agreed that it probably had to be someone related to one of the people they must have known back then. When asked if she knew anyone that had a child shortly after graduation, Denise thought about it a minute and said the only couple she remembered like that still lived in town, and the child was a daughter. She admitted that she had lost track of a lot of people over the years, but she promised she would think about it and call her back if she came up with any ideas.

Jaycee and Kate lay in bed six miles apart that evening thinking about the very same thing. Jaycee, rooted deep in logic, was going over the 'known' details and trying to make sense of someone, if he did have some connection to her, coming this far and not contacting her. She had no choice but to cling to the 'grand coincidence' theory; not that this boy didn't know someone, or wasn't related to someone that knew her in high school, but that he came by this area strictly by coincidence. After all, very few people from her home town knew she lived in this area, and not many of the locals would know that she and Kate's relationship was anything more than teacher/student.

Kate, with instinct firmly in control, was absolutely convinced that Elijah knew of their relationship. She had, after all, mentioned her favorite teacher. She couldn't remember if she actually mentioned Jaycee by name, but she distinctly remembered talking about her. Her last waking minutes were spent reviewing every word she could recollect from the conversations with him, as though she was searching for a puzzle piece.

Kate didn't get to tell Mallory the story until she saw her in school. It took most of the lunch break to fill her in on all the details, but Mallory was fascinated by the coincidence of it. When Kate asked her how she could be convinced that it was all just a coincidence with the same school, the name and the description of the stuff she wore to the prom, Mallory simply said that it had to be. "Why else," she reasoned, "would he be talking to you and not Jaycee herself?"

Mallory was quick to come to the same conclusion to which Jaycee kept returning. This boy, whoever he was, didn't attend a high school that closed something like eighteen years ago, so he may have told her the truth about a Josephine who he *did* like at whatever school he *did* attend. And, the navy blue dress, well, that *would* be a coincidence, but it wasn't as though it was a very rare prom outfit either.

Kate's only defense for such logic was that she was the one who talked to Elijah, and that there was something about him that she couldn't explain. Not very firm ground, she was well aware, for debate.

The following evening, as Kate focused the telescope on Vega, just as she was getting the adjustment right, she pulled her head back and gasped "the dog star!"

"Not at this time of night, sweetheart," her dad called from the kitchen table where he was enjoying some coffee while reading the paper.

"He called the dog star 'an opera in the sky', exactly as Jaycee did," she thought to herself. Mumbling something about the dog star being "his favorite" as she moved swiftly through the kitchen on her way to the phone to call Jaycee, Kate was stopped by her dad when he moved to block her path.

"What's this about the dog star, Kate?" asked her father. "And where are you going in such a hurry?"

"Nowhere, Dad," she answered innocently. "I just need to use the phone."

"And, what's wrong with the phone in here?" he inquired, pointing to the phone she had already passed.

Kate explained that she needed to ask Jaycee something, and she thought it would be easier to use the phone in her bedroom so as not to disturb his reading.

"Well, that's very considerate, sweetheart," he complimented her with a suspicious look on his face, "but you won't be bothering me a bit. You go right ahead and use the phone all you want."

In order not to seem too secretive, Kate thanked him, picked up the kitchen phone and dialed Jaycee's number. Knowing she wouldn't be able to discuss the topic the way she had hoped, she immediately began speaking in code as soon as Jaycee said "Hello."

"I was thinking about that comment you made about Sirius during our astronomy session," Kate blurted out without even a greeting.

"Something tells me this isn't about astronomy, right?" Jaycee guessed.

"I was just thinking how odd a description that is," continued Kate.

Confused, Jaycee paused thinking Kate would fill in the blanks. Realizing, after the silence continued, that Kate was either preoccupied or not *able* to say more she asked if there was a reason she was being so aloof.

"Yes," she said, "I was just wondering how many people would know that."

"Know about the dog star?" asked Jaycee, who was now playing along.

"Yeah, about that whole opera thing that you told me," Kate replied, feeling good that she was able to get her message out so discreetly.

"I take it someone *else* mentioned that?" Jaycee seemed surprised.

"Well, yes." she answered

"And you are being so vague, I'm guessing, because your dad is nearby?" Jaycee asked.

"Of course," Kate shot back.

"All right then, at least now I understand this game. To tell you the truth, I was going to call you anyway, Kate," Jaycee announced. "But, I figured instead I would just catch you in school tomorrow. If you have a few minutes to get together tomorrow afternoon, I'll run you home after school."

"Yeah, sure, no problem. I'll see you then, Jaycee." agreed Kate.

"Before you hang up, though," said Jaycee just as Kate was about to say goodbye, "are you telling me then that this boy mentioned something about Sirius being like an opera?"

"Absolutely!" She affirmed.

"Okay, Kate," Jaycee said sounding flustered. "But, I have to tell you, dear, you're not doing anything good for my dire need to get a restful sleep tonight. I'll talk to you tomorrow."

Before she got a chance to see Jaycee at school the following day, Kate found herself re-hashing the Elijah mystery with Mallory during lunch period. Mallory announced that she had discussed the whole thing with her mother, except for the sleeping over part. Kate's facial reaction was sufficient to alert Mallory to the fact that this wasn't interpreted as a particularly welcome piece of news. It was that exaggerated, closing of the eyes while looking down, thing that Mal had become familiar with over the years. But, before Kate could speak, she assured her that she had her mother's guarantee of secrecy.

Kate explained that it wasn't the secrecy that concerned her, even though she admitted that she would feel bad if her dad heard the "whole" story from someone else before she got a chance to bring him up to date. Although discussing it with her father *was* something she wanted to do, she felt the Elijah subject was still a little too sensitive with him since the sleepover confession, so she was carefully scouting the proper timing for that conversation.

The concern Kate had, she informed Mallory, was that she comes out looking like an irresponsible fool no matter how the tale was told. Having had time to give this thought, Kate knew that associating with this stranger at all would be seen as foolish by anyone who heard the story. She also knew that, since no one else could verify any of the conversations, it would be easy to shrug off many of the coincidences as misunderstood comments, or misinterpretations of what was said. Maybe some people, she feared, would even think she made the whole thing up.

Mallory, apologetic in her tone, assured Kate that no one that knew her would ever think she made up something like that.

"That's what makes it such a good story," Mallory confessed. "This is level headed Kate telling it. Anyway," she continued, "the reason I'm bringing this up is, my mother reminded me of a Bible story from the Old Testament she used to tell me when I was really young, about a prophet from this place called Gilead. It's kind of weird Kate, but *his* name was Elijah," she announced, craning her neck as if she had stumbled onto something really important.

"Mal?" Kate calmly called out. "You *were* listening when I told you about this guy that showed up out of nowhere. You *did* hear me when I said that he told me he went to a high school someplace that I found out *closed* a long time ago, and that he liked someone named Josephine who really *did* attend *that* particular school. Somehow this guy even knew what this Josephine wore to the prom, which apparently took place before he was born. Now, I couldn't help but get the impression that all of this you figured for coincidence, Mal, which is okay. But," she stopped to put both hands on Mallory's shoulders and looked directly into her eyes, "if I understand you now, because his name appears in the Bible, *that* makes it kind of weird. Are you out of your mind?" she jokingly shouted as she shook her to show her frustration.

At the end of 6th period, Kate headed down to Jaycee's classroom to meet her as agreed. Through the glass in the door, she could see Jaycee engaged in conversation with several students at the front of the room while she wiped down the chalkboard, so she decided to wait in the hall. When Jaycee came out, still in conversation with the three girls who were at the blackboard with her, she immediately noticed Kate standing against the wall and excused herself from the group by saying "let's pick this up in class tomorrow, ladies. I have to get going now."

Walking together to the car, they discussed Kate's recollection of the 'opera' comment. Jaycee admitted that, having had a chance to think about it, maybe it wasn't all that strange since, although she first heard it from a science teacher in her high school, it was possible that the teacher read it somewhere and was merely passing it along.

"I'll tell you, Kate, this whole thing has occupied more of my thinking time than I can afford. I just can't figure out why your friend mentions my high school and my name. This is crazy."

Kate told her that she couldn't get Elijah out of her mind. She attempted to assure her again, with the most serious look, that she was absolutely convinced that he was someone whose intentions were good, and that she was positive he would not have contrived all of this as some kind of a hoax. Kate looked at Jaycee seriously and told her that if she had any idea where she could find him she would have no second thoughts about going to see him, wherever it was.

"There's more to this than just the mystery then, hey Kate?" Jaycee turned and began walking again. "This sounds like it might be a love interest."

"I honestly don't know exactly how I feel, Jaycee," Kate said in a flustered tone. "It's so difficult to explain. I've just not met anyone at all like him. I mean, I've known him such an incredibly short time, and I'm not at all the type to warm up to people very quickly. It's not that I actually think of him as a potential boyfriend, but I know I could listen to him forever. He knows things, and he has such a gift for getting a point across. Sometimes it's like listening to a great teacher, like yourself Jaycee, only young. It's just...."

"Excuse me?" Jaycee interrupted acting as though she had been slighted. "Only young?"

"More like my age, Jaycee. You know what I mean. Of course I consider you young. Anyway, it's very strange, and I just feel like I need to know more about him."

Jaycee thanked her for the "great teacher" compliment, and accepted it on behalf of all the "elderly" teachers, as they got into the car. She told Kate that she respected her opinion, and could only hope that she would get a chance to meet the person deserving of such high praise.

In the eight days that passed since the after school conversation, Kate had become progressively less obsessed, albeit not in what would be considered very noticeable degrees, with the idea of finding out more about Elijah, at least during the day. In the evening, though, after the homework and barn duty, she still took out the map of the United States occasionally and looked at the arc she had drawn through the country, north to south, with her geometry compass. It was a line that represented about 1300 miles from where she lived, which she traced the evening after he left. She sometimes stared at the line as if something would occur to her from their conversations, which would give her an idea about where he was going. It was one evening during such a geographic pondering when she noticed through her bedroom window that there were headlights coming up the driveway. By the time she got to the window, Jaycee's Mustang was coming to a stop in the driveway in front of the porch.

"Hey, Kate!" her dad yelled from downstairs. "I believe we have some company."

Jaycee was just taking a seat at the kitchen table by the time Kate got there. "It's both hard *and* humbling for me to say, sweetheart, but the lady has come to see *you*," Her father said with a feigned tone of sadness.

To that, Jaycee promised that the next time she came by, it would be strictly to visit him.

As Kate sat at the table, her dad was offering coffee, which Jaycee accepted, and while confirming his recollection that she would take only a bit of cream in it, Jaycee fished a piece of paper from her purse and laid it on the table.

What Kate saw took her breath away for a moment. From across the table, even with the paper slightly folded, Kate could see the photograph on the front of the page. It was Elijah.

"Where….? How did you get this?" asked a shocked Kate.

Jaycee explained that her sister was in touch with a girl that lived close by when they were in high school. This girl was in the graduating class ahead of Jaycee's. The

Classical High class of 1969. When her sister asked her if she remembered anyone that was interested in Jaycee back in high school, she remembered a boy in her class that she was sure had a crush on the, then, Josephine. The copy of the photograph came from the yearbook. As Kate picked up the paper for closer inspection of the small picture, she noticed the name was Charles 'Chaz' Sanderson. Her face went pale as she lay the page back down on the table.

"I take it you recognize the features," Jaycee inquired. "Do you think this might be a relative of your Elijah?" With a voice slightly trembling, Kate answered, "No, I think this *is* Elijah!" and, just as her father delivered Jaycee's coffee, Kate got up and left the room.

As she ran upstairs, her father looked at Jaycee for some sort of explanation, but Jaycee didn't know where to start, and just as she felt obligated to make an attempt to say something which might explain Kate's quick exit, they could both hear her footsteps coming back down the stairs in as much of a hurry as when she had left.

Kate rushed into the kitchen with the guitar Elijah left for her, and held it out for Jaycee to see as she approached her.

"You see there under the strings?" she said sounding a bit out of breath. "You see the initials? This is the only thing he left behind."

"C.S.," Jaycee said out loud, feeling a slight chill as she read it. "Now, you didn't tell me about any guitar, Kate," she noted.

"No," Kate explained. "I didn't think this really meant anything. I guess I thought it was just initials from a former owner. What does it mean, Jaycee?" Kate asked with eyes wide.

"What does *any* of this mean?" her father interjected from behind the table. "Could somebody catch me up here?" he pleaded.

Jaycee decided to bring Michael up to date with the mystery surrounding Elijah. He hadn't even known the name. Kate had only referred to him as a boy who she met at the meadow when she confessed about the overnight visit. While Jaycee told the story involving the details of what she termed 'coincidences', Kate picked up the copy of the photograph once again and read the verse under the picture.

Charles 'Chaz' Sanderson

Quiet & shy,

this new boy in town.

Will miss most:

Cafeteria applesauce,

Smoking in the boy's room,

and the Goddess in Economics.

"I'm going to take a wild guess that you were in this boy's Economics class," commented Kate after reading the excerpt.

"Yes, I think that could be a reference to me," she blushed.

Jaycee looked pensive as she began to tell the story, which she said she remembered as soon as she received the copy of the yearbook photograph.

"In her letter," Jaycee said referring to the letter from her sister which accompanied the photo, "my sister reminded me of an incident at Classical High which I had long since forgotten. It involved this Charles Sanderson. As I told you, he was a senior when I was a junior so I really didn't know him except for that one class.

Near the end of the school year, just before he would have graduated, I remember hearing that he had gotten into this awful fight. Everyone was talking about it the next day because Charles had gotten arrested for hurting this guy pretty seriously with a knife. The guy he hurt didn't go to our school. I think he may have dropped out a couple of years before, but, he was pretty well known around the area as a bad seed.

Anyway, there were only two kids who said they saw what happened during the fight and, unfortunately, both were friends of the guy that got cut. They told the police that Charles actually pulled the knife.

He didn't return to school, but I remember I ran into him at a store after school one day and asked him how it was going. He said that it didn't look good because these two friends were willing to lie, and that he was, in fact, trying to take the knife away when the guy fell on his own blade. I felt really bad for him. I just knew he was telling the truth. I think I told him then that I believed him and that I hoped he would get a break. But, he didn't seem very hopeful.

Since he was almost eighteen at the time, and had apparently gotten into some minor trouble with the law before, when he went to trial the judge decided to make a deal with him. If he committed himself to the draft board for immediate service on his eighteenth birthday, the case would be dismissed. At the time, I guess I didn't realize that judges were offering that kind of choice regularly when they thought they were dealing with kids that could use the kind of discipline that the military could provide.

I did hear someone mention during that summer Charles had shipped out for basic training, and I guess I took that as good news. But I didn't really know anyone else that knew him very well, so I never really heard any more about him after that. And I sure never knew he liked me, though I do recall talking to him a few times in class before the trouble began. I didn't know anything about him, but I remember he surprised me when I *first* talked to him, because he seemed so nice, and he was so shy. It wasn't how I expected him to be because he looked like a pretty tough kid. I also remember thinking he seemed mature compared to most of the high school boys I knew. I guess I attributed that to him being a senior.

And that's what I know about Charles Sanderson," she finished.

"So," Kate injected as Jaycee paused, "if you cut this boy's hair and add a year or two to this face, it's Elijah. How do you explain that?"

"I'm sure now that this has to be," Jaycee advised while staring at the picture, "as we first thought, Kate. It's got to be somebody related to him. Someone who heard about me through him."

"And why," Kate began when her dad decided to interrupt.

Kate's dad sat at the middle of the kitchen table watching the conversation between Kate and Jaycee at each end as though it was Wimbledon. Still trying to sort out the 'coincidences' Jaycee relayed during the explanation, and keep up with what they were making of this new piece of evidence he decided he had no idea where Kate was headed with her theory.

"I think I may be lost here, sweetheart," her dad confessed, holding his hands just off the table as though signaling a time out. "Are you trying to say that this stranger you met *is* this boy in the yearbook, or is related to him somehow?"

"Believe me, Dad, I know there's only one sane answer to that," Kate admitted after a slight hesitation. "But, I just don't know what to think. This boy was different from anyone I ever met. He talked about things that I later found out had to do with Jaycee, like they were experiences of his own.

"I keep thinking that he should have been talking to her. Why would he come all this way and not see her. I just know that it wasn't some incredible coincidence that he ran into me out there at the meadow. That I know. And if I knew where he was right now, I would go there just to get the answer."

"He never mentioned, I take it, where he was off to then?" asked her dad.

With a quick "Not exactly," Kate left the room again and headed upstairs. This time when she returned she was carrying a large map. As she laid it on the table, she turned to Jaycee and reminded her about the 1300 miles he said he had to travel.

"I measured the 1300 miles from here with a compass and made this line as a possible range of where he was going," she announced.

"That's it?" her father asked, with a rather chagrined look. "The clue is that he was going 1300 miles? Why did he happen to tell you the distance and not the place?"

"He said he wasn't sure if what he needed to do might get him in some sort of trouble, so he was not comfortable sharing any details," she replied. "But, somewhere in the conversation, when he said he had to leave, he mentioned having a long way to travel. As a matter of fact he said '1300 hundred miles as the raven flies'."

"Raven?" her father and Jaycee asked, almost simultaneously.

"Yes, and when I corrected him I distinctly remember him saying something about the distance 'being the same with one black bird or another'."

Jaycee looked as though she was deep in thought. "I haven't read that story in a lot of years, but I wonder if he might have been telling you something with that reference," she said as though thinking out loud.

"I have it," Kate announced as she went to the living room and retrieved the book of Poe short stories from the bookshelf. "Some of these were required reading last year," she cited as she handed the book to Jaycee.

While Jaycee found her way to the right section of the book, she told Kate that she seemed to remember a reference to a place of some kind in the story. Tracing over the lines with her fingers, the room remained silent for almost a minute.

Her finger stopping at a section very near the end, Jaycee read the passage to herself and then recited:

> "On this home by horror haunted
>
> tell me truly I implore.
>
> Is there - is there balm in Gilead?
>
> Tell me - tell me, I implore!
>
> Quoth the Raven, nevermore"

"*Gilead?*" Kate shouted. "My God, Jaycee! *Gilead?*" she repeated as she stood up and put her hands on the table. "In the Bible *he's* from Gilead!" she proclaimed. "Mallory told me about the Bible story her mother used to read to her. It was about this prophet, Elijah, and he was from a place called Gilead. Maybe he told us where he's going, Jaycee! Maybe he told us where he is!" Kate said, her voice trailing as she knelt beside Jaycee.

Jaycee put her hands on both sides of Kate's face and looked in her eyes. "I don't know Kate, this is all so strange," she added with a tone of skepticism. "What if this Gilead is a fictional place? A biblical place?"

With that, Kate's dad went to the living room where Kate retrieved the Poe book, and returned with a much larger book. When he laid it on the table, Jaycee and Kate could see that it was a World Atlas. He searched the index with his finger as Jaycee had done with 'The Raven'. When he came to what he was looking for he looked up for a moment, mumbled the word "interesting", then looked back at the page, mouthed the page number and thumbed through the large book until he found it. After seeing what he needed to see in the book, he turned Kate's map toward him and studied it for a minute.

"Is it a real place, Dad?" Kate asked. "Is there a Gilead?"

"Well," he stated in a serious tone, "according to this Atlas there is only one place by that name in this country."

He turned the map so that Jaycee and Kate could see and, without saying a word, carefully placed his finger down in the middle of Indiana, almost at the exact intersection of the curved red line that Kate had drawn.

The silence that lingered for just under a minute was all the time necessary for anyone who had remained a skeptic up to that point to fashion a white flag.

Kate gazed at the place where he put his finger, wide eyed as a child on Christmas morning, while her father couldn't seem to take his eyes off the map, and Jaycee sat silently staring at the same point.

"I've got to get there, Dad!" Kate abruptly announced. "Somehow, I've got to get there. You *have* to understand. I know now that meeting him was not an accident. I have to ask him why he came here. Why he came to me."

"Hold on!" her father jumped in. "Let's not get crazy here, Kate. You can't just…. You have school! There's no way I could even think about allowing you to take off across the country to find this guy."

"I agree with your dad," Jaycee added. "As intriguing as this all is, you really can't be sure if he actually went there. Or, even if he did, there's no way of knowing if he would still be there, Kate."

"This whole story he told me about Galileo was for a reason," Kate said softly, looking away as if she were in deep thought. "He was making the point that it is important to stand by what you know to be true, even when those around you refuse to believe.

"I understand how crazy you both think that this is. I do. But, you didn't meet this boy, I did. And I have no doubt that he knew I would figure this out. He knew I would somehow get to where he is going. I don't know what I can tell you to make you believe me, but I've never felt more sure of anything in my life. Please trust me on this. I *have* to get there. I'm not exactly sure why, but I know I have to do this. I know I have to do this, and I'm begging you dad, please help me get there."

Having quickly nixed the idea by exercising the parental veto in the name of logic, Kate's father watched his daughter as she spoke about how important this was to her. There was a strangely familiar mix of sadness and determination in her eyes. His world and hers had been so closely intertwined these past 12 years, just as his and her mother's before she was born, that he suddenly knew exactly what she was feeling. He had seen the same look on her mother's face when the doctor told her that childbirth would be risky for her. This was not his little girl insisting on getting her own way. He could see that she was absolutely convinced that this was the right thing to do, and her sadness came from the fact that no one else could appreciate her conviction.

"You sound like your mother now, sweetheart," her father quietly reflected. "I suspect that's just the way she would have sounded. And I trusted her judgment enough to have probably even gone along with something this crazy if she was as determined as you seem to be right now. It's only right that I respect your judgment in the same manner.

"If it is that important to you, I am going to get you there, but you have to understand that I couldn't possibly be okay with letting you go on your own. Who knows what could happen?"

"Well, you two aren't going without me!" chimed Jaycee.

A long silence followed Jaycee's comment as each of the three looked to the other and then to the map. Such spontaneity is almost always followed by a moment of reason. But, the pact had been made, and so would the journey. The only member feeling less than excited about it at that very moment was Michael, though his understanding of how important it was to Kate helped him to disguise it adequately.

Studying the map together for the next hour to determine the best route, and how long such a journey would take, it was estimated that with Jaycee and Michael sharing the driving they could probably make it in about 22 hours or so, depending on stops, which made it a bit too long to do in a weekend.

"The weekend after this is a three day weekend at school." announced Jaycee. "If we left early Friday morning we could have most of Saturday there, turn around and get back sometime Sunday night. I'm pretty good driving long distance. I drove by myself coming out here from Massachusetts, and went through the night without any problems. But, I'm afraid my old car might not hold up on this kind of trip."

It was decided that the following weekend would be the time to go, and that the family van would best accommodate one or two people sleeping along the way.

As Jaycee was leaving that evening, she turned and hugged Kate's father, and thanked him for being so understanding of such an insane situation.

"It's a very special man that would do this for his daughter, Michael," Jaycee told him. "I know this whole thing sounds absolutely bizarre, but I have to admit, I think I'm looking forward to next weekend as much as Kate is. Maybe every now and then we have to be a little crazy. I don't know. I just think you're a Prince for helping us try to figure this all out."

She leaned and kissed him lightly on the lips before turning and walking quickly out the door. It surprised Kate as much as it did her dad.

"See you in school tomorrow, Kate!" she yelled back from the driveway as she opened the car door.

"See you tomorrow," Kate replied.

There was almost no sleeping that night for Kate. She was absolutely ecstatic about the idea of seeing Elijah again, and finding out what his connection was with Jaycee. While lying in bed thinking about how it might be when she found him, she thought of different things she might say. The possibility that she wouldn't find him didn't once cross her mind. She was well aware, though, that the next eight days would pass more slowly than most months.

Kate promised her father she wouldn't mention the trip to anyone, including Mallory. He convinced her that the fewer people that knew about such a strange mission, the fewer there would be to consider them totally out of their minds. But, not telling Mallory was about as hard a task as she could bear. Especially when she was with her over the weekend and asked directly why she seemed so preoccupied. Mallory at one point asked her if she was still thinking about this Elijah person, giving Kate an out, which she took by admitting that it was exactly why she seemed out of sorts.

At "The Rack" with Mal on Saturday night, Kate spent some time talking to Keith, who seemed to be trying to tell her something all night, but never quite getting to it. Toward the end of the evening he worked up the courage to ask her to the 'Fall Festival Dance', which was put on by the school. It was an annual semi-formal affair put on by the combined junior/senior class, considered to be second only to the prom in gala events for the school year. Unfortunately, however, it was to fall on the following Friday evening.

This was a tight spot. If she told Keith that she was going to be away, Mallory would definitely hear about it, and she wondered how *that* would be explained. The truth though, in a slightly exaggerated form, won out in the few seconds she had to think about it.

She explained to Keith that she had already promised her father that she would go on a trip with him, "a business trip of some kind", and he asked her along so they could see a couple of colleges that she was thinking about at the same time. She assured him, as best she could to spare his feelings, that she definitely would have accepted his invitation if she was going to be in town, though his dejected look told her that he was far from convinced.

Kate realized by his reaction that his feelings for her were sincere, and, for the first time she found herself appreciating the way he had always been so open about those feelings. Having paid such little attention to him all this time suddenly felt wrong. He had been very patient, and he seemed truly sensitive. It struck her that he was a lot like her in a certain way.

"I'll tell you what, Keith," she offered. "Since I'm going to be missing this big event, maybe we should plan to go to the Prom together well in advance. That way I know I won't forget and agree to do something else on *that* weekend."

Keith seemed both thrilled and shocked that Kate would ask *him* to the Prom. He knew that when the time came, he would find a way to ask her. There was no doubt about that, but he had already wondered how far ahead he would need to ask to be certain that he was the first.

"By the way, Keith," she smiled, "you don't by any chance have a car with one headlight out do you?"

"I don't even have a car," he replied with a confused look as he turned to head back toward the stage for another set.

Kate grinned and shook her head, momentarily reflecting back on the conversation with Elijah, as Keith walked away. "So much for the junker with one headlight," she mused to herself.

"All I have is a motorcycle!" he yelled back through the crowd.

Markers set in rows and rows
So still they lie, these broken boys
Come to rest they, come to rest these boys

Chapter Ten

The Drama

Friday morning, as expected, arrived more than a month later in Kate's mind. For several hours the night before, Kate sat idly by while her dad and Jaycee went over driving plans. But when Jaycee brought up the subject of music to take along, Kate jumped into the conversation.

"Why don't you bring your oldies tapes, Jaycee? *Please!*" she insisted while looking at her father with an impish grin.

After packing a few things to wear, and a cooler full of snacks, sandwiches and drinks, at 7:30 Friday morning, Kate and her father started out for Jaycee's.

"The adventure begins," Jaycee said as she got into the front seat of the van.

The sign on Route 64, which would take them through the Kiowa Grasslands and eventually into Amarillo, Texas, to join the interstate, read "Clayton 88 miles."

They celebrated reaching the highway, after more than four hours of back roads, by passing out sandwiches and cold drinks. Jaycee had studied the route enough to have memorized many of the historically significant areas, and kept pointing out things that they passed in an attempt to make the trip something of a learning experience for Kate.

Stopping to have dinner outside of Joplin, Missouri, Jaycee and Michael concurred on how they had managed to be ahead of the schedule they had estimated. While this was a relief, they knew there were long desolate stretches ahead as they diagonally crossed Missouri and Illinois.

After eating and filling the tank, Jaycee volunteered to take over the driving. She advised Kate and her dad to get some sleep as it began to get dark, and she would wake them when it was time to refuel, five or six hours up the road.

When Kate woke up, her father was driving again and Jaycee was sound asleep in the front seat. She noticed the sky was beginning to lighten as they passed a sign that read "Indianapolis 30 Miles."

After a quick breakfast at a "Bob Evans", and cleaning up as well as possible in the restroom after, the three climbed back in the van for what was thought to be the last few hours of the journey. It was 5:30 in the third time zone since the trip began.

The Indianapolis skyline reflected the pink hues of the dawn beautifully. From the highway it looked like a clean, modern city, which was still asleep.

Following the map off the main road, well north of Indianapolis, was a series of signs to towns that seemed to be named for any far away place; "Mexico", "Peru", "Chile", and finally, on a small two lane road in the middle of several large farms; "Gilead - 6 Miles".

For the first time, Kate contemplated the worst. "What if we don't find him?" she thought to herself. Unbeknownst to her, Jaycee was thinking the very same thing at that moment.

As they drove past the sign that read "Entering Gilead" on a long flat stretch of road, which seemed to give new meaning to the term 'middle of nowhere', Kate's dad pulled the van to the side of the road.

"One thing is pretty certain by the looks of this town," he commented. "If your Elijah is here, or came here, it shouldn't be difficult to find someone that knows about it. Did anyone have a plan, by the way, as to how we are going to go about looking for him?" he inquired.

Jaycee suggested they go further down the road to see what was actually in the town, and decide from there where might be the best place to begin asking about Elijah. She said she had imagined going to a police station or Post Office to ask, but it now appeared possible that the town contained neither.

Down the road was the "Gilead General Store", an old relic of Americana with a wide front porch and a screen door. Before getting out of the van, which Michael had pulled into the wide dirt drive at the front of the store, they realized it had not yet opened.

"It's only 7:45," Jaycee reminded her fellow passengers. "The sign says the store opens at 8:00."

Deciding to take a ride to see if there was any more to the town, Michael pulled the van back onto the pavement and slowly headed back down the road.

The first sign of life could be seen ahead in the form of a small boy walking along the side of the road. It was Saturday morning, and Jack usually showed up to help out at the store when they opened on Saturday.

When Kate suggested they pull up and ask the boy if he knew where they could find a police station, her dad refused.

"We're liable to panic the poor boy!" he insisted. "A van full of strangers pulling up in front of him out here, asking questions. No. I think we can wait for the store to open."

As they passed him, slowly, he stopped walking and turned toward them, watching curiously as they drove by.

In the instant that the vehicle moved past the boy, Jaycee gasped and yelled for Michael to stop.

"Jesus…. Oh Jesus! Stop the car Michael! Stop the car!." she screamed in a sudden panic.

Michael pulled the van to the side of the road immediately, causing the tires to skid in the dirt. Before he could even come to a full stop, Jaycee was already crying hysterically with her head in her hands. She was trying to speak, but couldn't manage to get out anything beyond "Oh my God!" which was difficult to distinguish through the uncontrollable sobbing.

Kate and her dad were momentarily frozen in fear by Jaycee's sudden outburst. It is the kind of moment that comes when one takes instant account of all that is going on at the same time. It is like being caught between what is real and what isn't. Waking up after dozing off for a fraction of a second while driving down a dark highway brings about this sort of heart pounding focus.

When Jaycee first made the sound that one makes when they take in a breath of terror, Kate instinctively gasped and held the back of her father's seat to brace for what she thought might be the sudden impact of an oncoming car. One that only Jaycee must have seen. Within a second, when it was clear that there was no crash forthcoming, her mind still numb, Kate tried to cry out Jaycee's name, but it came out as barely more than a whisper, which couldn't be heard above the muffled wailing.

As Jaycee pulled at the door to get out Michael reached over and grabbed her shoulders forcing her to turn and face him.

"Mi...chael......." She shrieked, still trying to turn for the door. "The face......Oh my God........it can't be......it can't be....... It's my... T.J!" she cried.

In the instant that the message registered with him, Michael felt every nerve ending fire in unison. His face turned ghostly white, and his grasp went limp. Jaycee easily pulled away and finally managed to get the door open.

Jack, now across the road and about 30 feet from the van, just stood there turned toward the stopped vehicle, curious about the skidding and the commotion. He had heard the woman yell "T.J." from inside, and it was a voice he somehow recognized, but found it frightening, and thought about turning and running. He wasn't sure what to think. He hadn't heard that name, or that voice since, well, since before his father told him that his mother had died. His dad told him that he would call him Jack, short for Jackson, from that point on. He told him that calling him T.J. would remind him too much of his mother.

In the momentary delay that caused Jack to pause and consider whether he should run toward the store or back toward home, he caught a glimpse of the woman coming around the front of the van. He didn't actually recognize her, but there was something very familiar about her, and he was sure he knew that voice.

She stood across the road looking at him, her chest heaving with gasps of emotion and tears streaming down her face.

"T.J.?" she called out, reaching her hands out toward him.

"Mom?" He found himself questioning, knowing full well that it couldn't be her.

As she ran toward him he noticed things familiar about her. The face, the hair and something in the way she stood, all a bit different from how he remembered her and, at the same time, so familiar. And by the time it first struck him that this really could be the person he remembered being his mother, it became impossible to utter a word due to the lump that had instantly formed in his throat. Tears immediately welled up in his eyes as he stood there in front of her with no idea what to do, and absolutely unable to move.

Kate jumped out and came around to her father's side of the van just as he was getting out. They watched together, in total awe, as the impossible scenario played out before them, their attention drawn back and forth from Jaycee to the boy and, within moments, they were both crying uncontrollably as well, as the reality of what was taking place began to sink in.

Jaycee ran across the road to hold her son. She dropped to her knees as she took him by his shoulders and looked closely at his face. "Oh God! My T.J.," she choked out. "You're all grown up."

They remained there, Jaycee holding him to her until Jack, unable at first to even close his outstretched arms around her, hugged her back as though he was making sure that she was real.

After several minutes, Jaycee stood and looked down to study the evidence of nearly six years of change in her son. She took his hand and lead him back across the road toward Michael and Kate, who were still each in awe of the spectacle they had just witnessed. "Michael, Kate," Jaycee said, still crying but considerably more controlled, "this is my son. I can't believe I'm saying this. This is my Timothy," she announced, and a hint of a smile developed on her face for just an instant, until she suddenly looked up and noticed that Kate was weeping as well.

Jaycee put her hand to her chest as if seizing control of her emotion racked body, still holding her son's hand with the other, and managed to speak with slightly more control as she looked at Kate.

"I don't know what it was that made you bring me here, sweetheart," she said reaching out to hug Kate with her one free arm. "I only know that I wouldn't be here without you. I love you, Katelynn! God bless you, Sweetheart."

In the next few minutes, as the emotions of the group began to slowly subside from an incomparable peak, Michael began to contemplate the sobering reality of the situation. Remembering that the boy had originally been kidnapped, he wondered if they shouldn't be getting to the Police immediately.

He bent down to speak to Jack, who had still not said a word.

"Is that where you live, Timothy?" he asked while pointing to the only house visible in the direction from which Jack was walking.

"Yes, Sir," Jack answered after looking at Michael long enough to be sure he was speaking to him, "That's Mr. Gilchrest's house."

"Uh huh," he smiled. "And your dad lives there too?" Michael nodded.

"No, Sir," Jack replied as he wiped his face. "He died."

Jaycee's face, the product of a tough night on the road followed by a bout of peaked emotion, now took on a dumbfounded look.

"Died?" she voiced looking down at Jack.

Bending down to look directly into Jack's eyes she questioned again; "Your father died?"

Jack slowly explained that his father died a few years ago, in a car accident near where they lived in Fort Wayne. And that *he* was put into a "group home", and then a Foster home, and then *another* group home for awhile before being sent down to live with Mr. and Mrs. Gilchrest.

Michael, now feeling less alarmed about the urgency to get to the Police, asked Jack and Jaycee together if it might be a good idea to visit with the Gilchrests.

"Jaycee, Timothy do you think we should maybe go over to talk to the Gilchrests?" Michael asked.

"My name is Jack, Sir!" he answered. "Jack Taylor."

"Your father kept the part of your name he liked the best," Jaycee told Jack as she bent down again and held both his hands. "He always called you Jackson when you were very small. Do you remember that, sweetheart?"

Jack confirmed that he did remember being called Jackson, and T.J., but not much more about life before he was told his mother had been killed in an accident, and moving away.

Upon reaching the Gilchrest house, Jack lead them in the front door, still holding onto Jaycee's hand, and introduced her to Mrs. Gilchrest as his "mother who was killed."

Hearing the whole story, about the abduction, and finally being convinced that Jaycee was really who she claimed to be, it was evident that Mrs. Gilchrest was sincerely excited for Jack. It was the first time that she gave him more than a cursory hug, and it was the first time that she considered how much she might miss him. This was only her second experience as a Foster parent, and although she had been through the classes and did her best to keep the recommended distance necessary to be a temporary parent, she had found it difficult to say goodbye to Pete when he was adopted, and knew now that it was going to be just as hard to see Jack leave.

She dug the emergency number of the Indiana Department of Social Services out of the desk drawer and suggested Jaycee start with them to find out what to do next.

The call to Social Services was long, and frustrating. It became painfully clear that nothing was going to happen until Monday, at which time a judge would need to be involved, and plenty of proof would be necessary to substantiate her story. For, as she was soon apprised, according to the records of the state of Indiana, this boy was Jack Taylor, not Timothy Jackson Turner as she claimed. The very red tape which was wound so tightly by the false papers that Jaycee's former husband submitted to get Jack into school was not going to be easily unwound. But even this apparent delay was seen by Jaycee as a minor inconvenience. There was nothing that could have dampened the joy she was feeling with this physical proximity to her child.

Later on, having asked Mrs. Gilchrest if they could take Jack out for awhile to have lunch together, they stopped by the General Store to meet Mrs. Wheaton and for Jack to apologize for not showing up to work. She was also in tears before Jaycee finished telling the story.

"Junior", Mrs. Wheaton admitted, was very special to her, and that she called him Junior because that was her own son's nickname when he was a boy, though he had long since "moved off to the city" and had kids of his own now. She was on her knees hugging Jack when she told him how much she would miss him, but how very happy she was for him.

"This is just unbelievable!" she kept repeating, and as she stood up to say goodbye, she made Jack promise to come by for a "proper send-off" before he left town.

As they walked out the screen door together, she told Jaycee that the short time Jack came by to help out after school was often the highlight of her day.

Michael had, meanwhile, made the decision that Jaycee would not make the trip back with he and Kate, knowing that she probably felt obligated to do so. He suggested that they ride back to Kokomo, which was the last town that he could remember passing through that might have a hotel and car rental agency, have lunch there, and get her situated for her stay. Jaycee, giving the matter some thought, decided that her sister probably could do the necessary running around back in Massachusetts on Monday for the notarized papers that she would need, and since she could hardly even think of the idea of leaving Jack, if even for a few days, agreed that she would stay.

At lunch, it was Jack who asked his mother if she wasn't dead, why she didn't come find him.

"Well, my sweetheart, that is a very long story, but for now I can tell you that I did look for you, everywhere I could think of looking. I missed you so much, you cannot know."

"And finally you came here," Jack added

"That is the very strange thing here, TJ, we actually came to Gilead to find someone else."

In all the excitement, she had not given any thought to the original reason for their trip.

"It is really hard to explain to you now," she began, "but Kate met someone that somehow, I think, knew we had to come here. I don't think I can make it so you could understand, because I sure don't. Best we can hope is that one day this Elijah will come back to explain it all," she said while she held his head against her.

"You know Mister Elijah?" he asked, to everyone's surprise.

While Jack explained his encounter with Elijah, Kate hung on every word. She felt at once excited that someone else could bear witness to his existence, and incredibly relieved that she might see him again. Although no one had really questioned her 'story' throughout this experience, she felt uncomfortable knowing that it was only *her* recollection of the casual conversations with this stranger that lead to this cross country adventure.

Jack expressed some concern about Elijah returning as he had promised and not finding him there, and that Elijah had promised to bring a Ted Williams card with him when he came back.

Jaycee told him that the only card left behind, because it was in a frame, when his dad ran away with him was the Ted Williams card, and that she saved it all these years to remind her of him.

Kate, having listened to Jack's concern about Elijah returning to Gilead and not finding him, assured him that what she had now come to know about Elijah gave her total confidence that if he wanted to find Jack again, he certainly would. She told him that Elijah had talked about him when he was with her, and that she could tell he cared deeply about him. She explained that she was pretty sure that Elijah was doing what he could to get him to stay where he was, just as she was sure he was doing all he could to get his mother to come for him, which, she said, was what he must have been somehow trying to arrange the whole time.

Kate and her dad said goodbye to Jaycee and Jack later that afternoon, having helped Jaycee find a rental car and a place to stay while she would take care of the business of reclaiming her son from the State of Indiana. Michael assured her that he would have no second thoughts about coming back out to get her whenever she was ready to return. But, she told him that she had thoughts of her and Jack flying out to Massachusetts first, to visit with her family, before heading back to New Mexico.

Michael and Jaycee hugged for several minutes with no words spoken before he turned to get in the van. Jaycee was in tears again by the time she tried to say goodbye to Kate. She knew that it would be impossible to express how she felt, so she just held Kate's face in her hands and fashioned a pained smile, while Kate said, "You hurry back!" through her own tears.

The return trip was more leisurely than the trip out. Michael decided after driving only six hours that a hotel, with a hot shower and soft bed, would be in order for the evening, so it was determined that Kate would probably have to miss school on Monday.

At one point during the trip the following day, somewhere in Oklahoma, Kate asked her father if he thought she would ever see Elijah again. After thinking for a moment, he admitted that he had wondered about that also, and he had the feeling that Elijah, whoever that really was, had accomplished what he came to do, and might not have a reason to return. She chose to hope he was wrong.

Jaycee phoned Kate from Massachusetts almost a week after she and her dad got back. She called to let her know that things went slowly, as expected, with the state offices, but with the assistance from the Massachusetts State Police, and even the F.B.I., she finally received custody of her son, and was visiting with her family. She told Kate that she expected to be back within a week, and looked forward to seeing her.

Kate noticed in the conversation that Jaycee seemed almost sad. When she asked her if everything was okay, Jaycee attributed her lack of enthusiasm to being tired from the fight with Social Services, the travel and the emotional shock. But, for someone who had been on top of the world just five days earlier, Kate thought she sounded troubled. Ten more days passed before Jaycee phoned one evening to let her know that she was back, and asked if she could come by to visit for just a few minutes. When she arrived, both Kate and Michael were quite surprised to not see T.J. with her. Kate had actually looked forward to the chance to ask him more questions about his conversations with Elijah.

"Where's the little guy?" asked Michael once Jaycee was in the door. "Oh, I couldn't bring him," she announced. "I'll tell you all about it. Can we sit for awhile?" The answer, and the tone, left both Kate and Michael wondering what was happening. They both figured she surely wouldn't have left the boy at her house alone. She couldn't even bear the thought of not being with him just two weeks before. Kate remembered how she sounded on the phone and began to wonder if something had gone wrong with the custody process.

When they were seated in the kitchen, Michael offered the coffee that he had prepared while she was on her way. Jaycee accepted the offer and, once poured, she began by apologizing to Michael for leaving him "high and dry" on the drive back. She admitted that she felt guilty about that when she was finally able to think more clearly. He assured her that it was the only way he would have had it in that situation, and that he and Kate made a longer, more leisurely, ride of the return, so it wasn't much of a hardship.

"I want to first talk about Elijah," she started in a serious tone, while looking directly at Kate. My sister and I did some searching for this Charles Sanderson while I was home. We learned, after finding no Sandersons in town, that he was a Foster child when he was at the high school my sister and I attended. We were able to get his old address from a state agency, thanks to my recent experience in dealing with this kind of matter. It turned out that the Foster family that Charles lived with was still at the same address, so we visited with them, to ask if they might be still in touch with him, or know where we could find him, and to ask whether they knew if it was possible that he could have had a son.

His Foster parents," she continued, "were so genuinely happy to talk about 'Chaz', as they said he liked to be called. He lived with them for almost three years before joining the military on his eighteenth birthday. They told us that they were sure he did not have a son before he left for the service, and, that he was killed in Viet Nam less than a year later." She paused to look up at Kate, who was sitting calmly with her hands folded in front of her. Jaycee, expecting an emotional reaction, reached across and put her hands on top of Kate's as a comforting gesture, and continued;

"He was an adult by then, of course, but since he listed his Foster parents as the next of kin, they were officially notified by the Army of his death. He died in the vicinity of Quang Tri, on December 5th, 1970."

"He died on the day I was born!" Kate said softly, her head nodding up and down slowly as if she was affirming a suspicion.

"Apparently so," Jaycee confirmed. For a minute no one spoke. Then Kate looked at Jaycee and asked "Did you ask about the guitar by any chance?"

"The guitar?" Jaycee sounded surprised.

"The one I showed you, with his initials on it. Did you ask about it?" she pressed.

"I knew what you meant, Kate. I was just kind of surprised by the question in light of what I just told you."

"I've had plenty of time to think over all that has happened," explained Kate. "It's obvious to me that I was given a message which was intended to somehow get you to where T.J. was. And it sounds like T.J. was given a message to stay put until you came to get him. You and I decided we were going to find this messenger. But, I guess down deep I never believed that we were looking for someone that knew someone who knew you Jaycee. I heard that boy sing *your* name. And I saw his eyes flash when he mentioned the details of what *you* wore to your Prom. Why he came to me is the question that haunted me," Kate admitted as she leaned back in her chair contentedly. But, he told me about these connections in life, and he told me that most are unexplainable. He also told me, in an indirect way, that I needed to be open minded to things that didn't seem to fit with all that I thought I knew.

"I'm not sure of the answer. Maybe the fact that I came into the world as he was leaving. Maybe I was more open to listening to what a stranger had to say, and maybe I don't even *need* to know. Something incredible happened here, though, and we were all a part of it. That's enough for me.

"So," she began again after a slight pause, "Yes! I would really like to know about the guitar." Jaycee leaned forward and confirmed that she did, in fact, ask the Foster mother if Charles had owned a guitar, and was told that he played the guitar almost constantly while he lived there.

"His Foster mother told me that she shipped it to him in Viet Nam, as he had asked, a few weeks after he got there. But, that it was not among the personal effects the Army had shipped back to her. She really did seem glad to have someone ask about him after all these years. It was pretty obvious that she was quite attached to him. She insisted I take this photograph with me when I left, so I accepted it thinking that you might like to have it." Kate looked at the photo, which appeared to have been taken while he was in Viet Nam. He was wearing jungle fatigues, sitting on a log playing the guitar, not unlike the log at the meadow, and very much like the guitar that was in her room. The likeness to Elijah, she thought, was uncanny.

The other thing I came to talk about, to tell you actually, is very difficult for me," she said in an alarmingly morose tone of voice. "The real reason that T.J. isn't here is that I needed to get him into school right away." Jaycee was fidgeting with her fingers and staring down at the floor while she was talking.

"Well, while we were back home I decided that he should have the chance to enjoy the rest of his family after all this time…..and out here, well, ……as much as I….."

"Oh God, Jaycee! This isn't…. You're not telling us you're leaving?" a stunned Kate interrupted.

"Kate, please," Jaycee responded. "Please try to understand. You can't know how hard this is. But, T.J. was, *is*, a part of my family, and not just mine and Bill's alone. He has an aunt, grandparents, cousins. I know that he needs to have those now more than ever. It's the only thing to do."

"You know, Jaycee," Michael finally spoke, smiling, in an attempt to stem the tide of what looked to have the potential to be another emotional scene, "when I first met you that day at the Big Sky, you might have given me some warning about the emotional roller coaster you had planned for me."

Jaycee tried to convey how hard it was for her to come to the decision to move back home, partly because she came to love the west, as she always suspected she would, and partly because she loved her job, but mainly because she had become so close, in such a short time, to the three of them.

"Three?" questioned Kate.

"I can't see bringing Duchess back to Massachusetts," Jaycee reluctantly admitted.

She went on to explain how things began to fall into place almost as soon as she arrived back home; that her sister told her about a teaching opportunity, a *science* teaching opportunity she emphasized, at one of the suburban high schools; and that a friend of her dad's had just retired and was in the process of moving out of a house which she had always loved, and offered to rent it to her if she was interested.

"I've just been so happy for you these past couple of weeks, Jaycee, that I don't think the fact that I really will miss you a lot can even dampen my spirits," announced Michael, still trying to lighten this devastating news for Kate's sake. It was already tearing at him inside to think that Kate would feel as though she was losing a mother figure again. He felt that they had become that close. "There is no question in my mind, though," he continued, "that you are doing the right thing. His grandparents have lived long enough without that boy." As he finished speaking, with as genuine a smile as he could muster, he looked over to Kate with the hope of seeing some acknowledgment of what he said, his heart still breaking for her.

Kate sat there, expressionless, staring down at the table, appearing to be deep in thought.

"Kate?" Jaycee said softly, trying to summon a response. "You aren't angry with me are you? I absolutely hate the fact that I have disappointed you, Kate. Please tell me that we can stay close, even with the distance. I can't tell you how important you are to me."

"Dad's right, Jaycee." Kate finally spoke in a surprisingly confident voice. "The joy that I have felt for you these past days, and knowing how happy your son will be around his own family again, well, I have actually broken out in tears a couple of times since coming back, just thinking about how good I feel about what happened,"

Kate stopped for a moment to look up at Jaycee, and within an instant of their eyes meeting, Jaycee's chin twitched slightly as the muscles in her face tightened in a desperate attempt to restrain her emotion.

"I can't be sad for myself, Jaycee," Kate went on. "And I know we will always be close."

Jaycee, tears now streaming down her face, got up from her chair and went over to kneel beside Kate. She hugged her without saying anything.

Michael, watching the two of them, was taken with an almost overwhelming sense of pride. He realized that Kate would be fine, and was suddenly aware of how much she had grown up these past months.

"Look here, my best friend," Jaycee said to Kate as they finally separated, "I have a proposition to discuss with you before I go." She explained that she wanted to buy Kate a ticket to come to Massachusetts during the week between Christmas and the New Year holidays. She told her that she had decided to go to Washington, to visit the Viet Nam Veterans Memorial, and she wanted Kate to go with her.

"We can drive down there during that week if you come out to visit," Jaycee pleaded.

Kate looked at her father with a tempered look of excitement.

"I know exactly what you are thinking, Little Miss!" her father spoke before she got the chance. "What will poor old Dad do if I'm gone? Well, to tell you the truth, if I can get someone to take care of the horses for a few days, I think I might just drive over to Las Vegas for a couple of nights that week. I've been wanting to get out there for awhile now, so please, sweetheart. You really should go."

"I guess I'll be there!" Kate smiled back at Jaycee.

Jaycee left that day feeling better than she thought she would. She spent the next day making arrangements for movers to ship her things back to New England. Kate, on the other hand, was feeling more than a little out of sorts the next day, and particularly downhearted when the announcement was made in school that Jaycee had begun an immediate leave of absence. Even though she was obviously aware of Jaycee's leaving, she was taken somewhat by the suddenness of it. Without having given the transition much thought, she somehow expected to see her at school for at least a few days before the actual move. The idea of not seeing her at all was beginning to settle, and it left her feeling much less stoic than she had pretended to be the prior evening.

From the school bus window, as it was approaching her stop that afternoon, she spotted the white Mustang in her driveway. She was instantly excited about the prospect of talking to her friend again before she left. As the bus pulled to a stop, and she was able to see the whole driveway, she noticed her father's van was not around, so she thought perhaps that Jaycee might be have come to say goodbye to Duchess.

Curiously, when Kate checked the barn there was no sign of her. And having looked over to the porch on her way she didn't see her there either. "Where else could she be waiting?" she wondered. It wouldn't be like Jaycee to enter the house with no one home, unless. "Sure!" she quickly deduced. "Dad was probably home when she arrived and invited her to wait in the house until I got home," she thought.

When she got to the stairs of the porch, she saw an envelope standing against the lamp on the table, and as she walked over to inspect it more closely she saw her name, in familiar handwriting, on the outside. Inside was a letter from Jaycee, explaining how her emotions had been worn thin over the past weeks, and that she was sure it would be too difficult to say goodbye in person. She thanked Kate, and told her how indebted she felt to her for "following her heart," and helping her to find the most precious thing in her life, and that she was absolutely sure that they would always remain the best of friends. As a small token of her appreciation, Jaycee was leaving her Mustang behind for Kate to enjoy. "I have had it long enough, and it is time for someone younger to enjoy it," she wrote.

The note ended, "Hope to see you soon. With all my love and gratitude, Jaycee."

Kate took her very first flight, Albuquerque to Boston via Chicago, the day after Christmas to visit as she promised. She went along with Jaycee and her son to the Memorial in Washington, and she brought the guitar with her. She left it leaning on the granite panel midway along the east wing of the chevron shaped sculpture, just below where she had traced his name onto a piece of paper. On the face of the guitar were the words she had etched with her father's wood burning tool:

"For Elijah

With Love,

Kate, Josephine and Jack"

As Kate walked Sanchez back across the meadow, she was thinking about how much had been going on in her life in the eight years since the trip to the Memorial. Having given birth to a son of her own during the past year had caused her to reflect back to this place often. For as much as Kate appreciated the incredible miracle she witnessed when Jaycee was reunited with her son, thanks to a stranger she met at this very place, it wasn't until she had a child of her own that she began to have any real appreciation for the unthinkable possibility of living without him. This made her all the more grateful that she was able, perhaps even chosen, to be a part of that miracle. Stopping at the place where her and Elijah once sat together, she tacked the note and a package of Twinkies in the very same place as the one that let him know she couldn't make their rendezvous on 'S.A.T.' day back in high school. If it happened that he came by again one day, he would know that she still thought of him. She lead Sanchez to the edge of the path leading out of the meadow, and turned back to look once more before leaving. As she did she could almost perfectly picture Elijah sitting on that log playing his guitar. She paused there a moment to wonder if he knew that she and Jaycee and Jack had made the trip to the Memorial, and she wondered if he knew how often she spoke of him over the years. She had once read the line; "Dead men live on the lips of the living", and decided to make certain that 'Chaz' would be talked about for as long as she could speak.

"Well, I guess that's all the reminiscing we have time for, old boy." she said to Sanchez as she hopped aboard and prompted him back down the path. "Dad will be looking for us soon."

She had told her father that she would be back in time for an early dinner with he and his grandson before she headed back home to Albuquerque. She was looking forward to telling him about the article in the paper, which prompted this spontaneous visit. It was an announcement regarding the dedication of a new museum in Washington, D.C., which would display all of the mementos left at the Viet Nam Veterans Memorial over the years. The moment she read it, she knew that one day perhaps when her son was old enough to understand the story about how the guitar got there, she would see the museum with him. By then, she thought, he would be aware of how she came to choose Elijah for his name.

CPSIA information can be obtained
at www.ICGtesting.com
Printed in the USA
FFOW01n1319180217
32563FF

9 781440 103483